RAKING THE ASHES

RAKING THE ASHES

Anne Fine

BANTAM PRESS

LONDON · TORONTO · SYDNEY · AUCKLAND · JOHANNESBURG

TRANSWORLD PUBLISHERS
61–63 Uxbridge Road, London W5 5SA
a division of The Random House Group Ltd

RANDOM HOUSE AUSTRALIA (PTY) LTD
20 Alfred Street, Milsons Point, Sydney,
New South Wales 2061, Australia

RANDOM HOUSE NEW ZEALAND LTD
18 Poland Road, Glenfield, Auckland 10, New Zealand

RANDOM HOUSE SOUTH AFRICA (PTY) LTD
Endulini, 5a Jubilee Road, Parktown 2193, South Africa

Published 2005 by Bantam Press
a division of Transworld Publishers

A catalogue record for this book is available
from the British Library.
ISBN 0593 054121

Typeset in 12/14.5pt Garamond 3 by Falcon Oast Graphic Art

Printed in Great Britain by
Clays plc, Bungay, Suffolk

1 3 5 7 9 10 8 6 4 2

Papers used by Transworld Publishers are natural, recyclable products
made from wood grown in sustainable forests. The manufacturing processes
conform to the environmental regulations of the country of origin.

For R.C.W.

1

GEOFF DROVE FROM THE WEDDING IN MUCH THE SAME MOOD HE would have left a funeral. It was obvious something had died. In the end, I decided it must be his sense of closeness to his son, that firm belief of his that, however rarely the two of them might see each other, however long the intervals between one or the other of them picking up the phone, there had been between them some unsnappable – even unshrivelling – bond. He'd been gung-ho enough on arrival. 'So there you are, Harry! Sneaking one last cigarette before the execution? And where's your bonny bride?' But from the way he'd taken to hovering in the background throughout the reception, I couldn't help suspecting his confidence was draining away. And, by the time the grotesquely balloon-clad limousine finally cruised off down the drive, Geoff was standing shyly on the edge of the gravel looking rather as if he felt he meant no more to his son than any of the overdressed, over-excited guests who milled after the car, waving.

I, on the other hand, was in the merriest of moods. Even after we got stuck in a traffic jam at Reading, I was pursing my lips every few minutes to imitate the lady in the hat with the flowers dancing on wires. 'In the summer, I am virtually a *fruitbat*!'

After another fifty miles or so, this clearly became tiresome. Geoff said accusingly, 'You had a good time!'

'I did.' I couldn't help snorting. 'And I don't think I've ever enjoyed a misprint more.'

Even forlorn Geoff had to chuckle. Most of the congregation had been singing with singularly little commitment. (Such a wet little hymn. I certainly never expected to have to warble it again after leaving my primary school.) And then we'd reached the small, unmissable, printed mistake:

> *He gave us lips to tell*
> *How great is –*

'Gold Almighty!' I crowed, and fell about laughing. I'd had a really good day. Something had vanished for me too; but what was gone was that humiliating sense of always being on the edge of things with Geoff and his children – as good as invisible sometimes: the stepmother who could be taken into account or ignored as inclination chose.

For we were both sidelined now. Geoff had his first salutary inkling of how I'd so often felt when word came – through Minna, not Harry – that the wedding would be in the first week of June.

I'd stopped on my way from the kitchen. 'What, before the eighth?'

Geoff gave me a look, but said nothing.

'It's the week of the inspections,' I said, not because I thought for a moment he might have forgotten, but to galvanize him back into speech. 'You know they're always at the start of June.'

'I'll ring Harry tomorrow.'

'You can't do that. We haven't even been invited yet.' To stop him trying to pre-empt me ('Oh, Tilly! Of course we're invited!'), I'd pressed on in a rush: 'You can't go telling them to change the dates for something you still only know about by accident.'

The father in him reared up, offended. 'Scarcely by accident!'

'I don't see what else you'd call it. It's not as if Harry's had the courtesy to ring up and ask, after all. "Oh, by the way, Dad, Tara and I are thinking of getting married. Would this date be all right for you and Tilly?"'

Now Geoff was turning sullen. 'So are you saying I should just let them carry on with the arrangements as they are now?'

'I think that's best. After all, *you* can still go. And it won't be the first time I'll have missed a family occasion.'

He couldn't fail to notice the veiled attack. 'Well, I am going to ring them.'

'No.'

'Now you're just being silly.'

And that was the cat out of the bag. 'Don't call my feelings "being silly", please. Your son's wedding matters to you, but my pride matters to me and I don't want you phoning on my account. If it's their choice not to check dates with me, it's equally my choice not to have you ring them.'

Geoff sounded so uneasy. 'Look, I expect they just didn't think about it.'

'How would they not think about it? Harry knows my job. He knows that once a year I go off on inspections and that the schedule is set in stone. If he was bothered, he'd have phoned to check.'

'Surely I could just mention it . . .'

On any other matter, I might have been more conciliatory. ('You must do as you like, Geoff. He's your son, not mine.') After all, the sheer bloody rudeness of the oversight had come as no real surprise. Right from the start, every last one of the Andersons had treated me as if I were some pleat in their family economy – there to be taken in and then let out again just as it suited them. But weddings are different. A wedding is a public event, and if you're not there it shows. ('I thought the young man had a stepmother. Has she not come?') The clear indifference behind their carelessness drove me to snapping. 'Oh, for Christ's sake, Geoff! Haven't you learned yet that, in a family like this, there's no such thing as "simply mentioning" something?' And it was true. I could have pointed to a million instances over the years, from way back when grave little Harry, swinging his legs tensely under the kitchen table, just happened to mention, 'Mum doesn't really like it when Tilly does our washing,' right through to Minna's recent greeting on the phone. 'Oh! Hi, Til. I thought you'd still be up in Aberdeen.'

In the end, of course, what with the blow-out off Troendseim, all the inspections were delayed. (No one to fly us out.) Head Office agreed we could vanish. The blokes went off climbing. I thought of joining them, but in the end decided that would be too close to staying in a sulk. Instead, I made the effort to cadge a flight back. I picked up a rather smart dress in Newcastle on the way home, and, by the time Geoffrey and I set off for Sussex the next morning, I was as free as anyone to celebrate the beginning of Tara and Harry's life together.

And start looking forward to the end of our own.

2

I WAS STILL MARRIED TO BILL WHEN I MET GEOFFREY. THINGS had been sticky from the start, and I had lovers – one after another – cheerful, juicy lovers who swept me out to concerts and films and restaurants. I can't remember ever having to step behind a pillar or bury my face in a menu till someone who knew me had passed. I think it must be that great long conveyor belt that runs from antenatal classes and nursery groups right through to school and teenage-party car pools that sucks most people into the community.

Women like me can dance all over that. And Bill wasn't 'social'. In fact, he was a grump. When he was home, I often found myself counting the hours till he went back on the rig; and I'm quite sure that he was happier watching films with the lads in those great floating cages than sitting morosely back home with me. Later, when I was working in oil too, I'd often meet people who worked with him. 'Great chap, Bill,' they'd tell me. 'Bundle of laughs. *Marvellous* sense of humour.' For quite a while, I took it all as tongue in cheek. But gradually I came to see that, just as I can be sweet and soft and uncritical in someone else's bed, in someone else's life, so Bill could be a warm and cheerful bloke away from me, and I felt better, rather than worse, for ratting on our marriage regularly.

By the end, we had the timings that worked best for us. He'd do his three weeks on the rig and, when he came home, I would as often as not be tossing my clothes into the bag for my next trip, or yet another course. And (what with the lovers) I managed to keep going. I don't have friends. Even way back in school, I'm supposed to have had a grudging attitude towards company my own age. Once, in a flu epidemic, I came home beaming. 'Good day?' my mother asked me. 'Brilliant!' I admitted. 'Almost everyone was off.' One of my many 'step-fathers' once asked me, rather pointedly, 'Is there a single one of your so-called "friends" you actually *like*?' And now I think about it, looking back, I do see what he meant. I chose my companions always because they interested me, never for any more soft-hearted reason. So some were sullen. Some were volatile. And some were downright mad. (Beth put her fingers in a switched-on blender and was off school for weeks.) Some were from families that made my mother's hair curl. None of them lasted as friends, and when I went to university I took up mostly with boys. For one thing, back then women were so rare in engineering that any girl could be a queen. And for another, I'd lost my nerve with my own sex. My last attempt at friend-ship with a girl broke down in our first year. Sarah knocked on my door, and then, instead of sitting on the rug in front of the

gas fire as usual, made a short speech. 'I've just come from my
therapist. And I was telling her that every time I come away
from you I somehow feel worse, as if you'd secretly amused
yourself by seeing how many little things you can slip into the
conversation to make me feel bad.'

'What on earth—?'

'No! Don't interrupt. You know exactly what I'm talking
about. All your mean, sneaky ways of coming back to the
fact that I can't do the work as well as you, and you have
more boyfriends. Why, you've even managed to make me
embarrassed about the way my jaw clicks when I'm eating
apples. And isn't it odd how the fact that my brother has been
in jail keeps coming up whenever we're—'

'That's bec—'

'No!' Sarah lifted an imperious hand. 'Me and my therapist
have—'

It was an open invitation to scorn. 'You and your therapist!'

'See! There you go again, trying to make me feel crap!' She
kept right on, though by now I was pushing her towards the
door. 'My therapist thinks that's all you want your friends for
– to make yourself feel bigger by putting them down, and
amuse yourself sticking in your little pins of spite.'

I slammed the door shut in her face. But clearly, having
mastered her valedictory address, she was determined to finish.
'So that's it, Tilly!' she shouted through the woodwork. 'I don't
want to be friends with you any more because it's not working
for *me*.'

Nor for anyone else, after that. It wasn't clear to me how

much the girls on my corridor had overheard, or how much Sarah had told them. But certainly everyone started to treat me with that unfailing courtesy that doubles as distance. I just got on with my work. It meant I got a better degree than most people round me, and solid praise from my tutors. So you could argue Sarah did me a giant favour, dumping me like that. And certainly I've never felt any gaping hole in my life where women friends ought to be. I married stupidly young – at twenty, if you can believe it; I myself scarcely can – and, what with Bill and my work and my lovers, I was busy enough.

Then I met Geoffrey. He was sitting on the beach with two miserable children. The wind was bitter. The toddler was howling, and the bigger one was whining hard. I walked past twice, and then my curiosity got the better of me and I walked past again. 'Why don't you take them up to one of the cafés?'

'I'm waiting for someone,' he told me.

'Their mother?'

He nodded.

'She'll have the sense to go and search up there, surely?'

He gave me one of those 'Well, you-don't-know-her, do-you?' looks, and I realized he must be a Sunday father. I felt great pity for him. 'Look, I'll stay here,' I offered. 'I'm dressed for it.' (You don't visit North Sea rigs, even in summer, without picking up warm togs.) 'You tell me what she looks like, and if she comes I'll tell her where you are.'

And that's what I did – sat on the beach and let the wind spit spray into my face while he took his caterwauling kids up for hot chocolate. I probably saved all their lives. When he came back, I gave him my number. 'In case you ever need some help again.'

That night I told my lover, who was a fat and easy Jewish businessman who loved his wife, 'I rather think I might have met your replacement today.'

'Where? At the dock office?'

'On the beach.'

'What were you doing *there*?' he asked, rather as if I'd said I'd met the man down some sewer. (In my experience, Jews aren't outside-y people.)

'I was taking a walk.'

'Where?'

'Nowhere.' I tried to explain again. 'It was a *walk*.'

And that was that. Sol didn't even ask, 'What was he like?' or 'Who was he?' So, what with not getting to say the name Geoffrey aloud, I quickly forgot it, and for the next couple of years simply thought of him from time to time as 'the man with the frozen children'.

Then I bumped into him again at some old flame's party. He was in the corner, alone and almost hidden by two tall leafy plants standing sentry on either side of him. 'How are the kids?' I asked.

'Fine,' he said, cheerfully enough. And then, because he didn't press on with something as general as, 'The older one's in nursery now,' or, 'The baby's finally grown some hair,' I realized he didn't have a clue where he had met me. Perhaps the last time I'd seen his kids was at the younger one's christening. On the other hand, maybe I'd stuck a needle in one of them at the Health Centre that morning.

'We met on the beach,' I reminded him. 'About three years ago. I gave you my phone number and you never rang.'

I waited, but nothing was forthcoming. So, as a bit of a flirt, I asked, 'Why didn't you ring? Didn't you fancy me?'

I knew he remembered me now. He was staring. 'You look completely different.'

'I'm wearing a whole lot fewer clothes, and my hair isn't sticking out sideways in the wind.'

And after that we danced, and I went home with him. (It wasn't one of his nights with the children.) We had a good time. In the morning I gave him my number again, and this time he rang it.

It turned out the party-going wasn't typical. He was a real home-bird. It wasn't long before he got in a stew about me still sleeping with Jerry (or Stefan or whoever – Sol was long gone by then) and started nagging me to take up properly with him.

I didn't mind. We got on really well. The weeks flew by. I met the children again. (Harry wasn't nearly so whiny, and Minna was sweet.) I thought I went down rather well with them, and so did Geoffrey. All the green lights were flashing. I think the end of it was quite inevitable. I can't remember ever being more content. One night, when maybe both of us had drunk a little too much, he asked me to move in. I made the effort of rolling over in the bed to look at him, so nice and rumpled and warm and friendly.

And I was mad enough to think, Why not?

*

In the end it was Geoffrey who moved in with me, because Bill had moved out and my place was much nicer. Ending my marriage turned out to be a hundred times more easy than I'd feared. I stalled for a month or two, then made a point of altering my schedule so Bill and I had three days in the house at the same time. I fed him home-made lasagne to weigh him down, then raised the subject of my 'recent straying'. (I was trying to be tactful.) But it turned out, to my astonishment, that Bill had had a mistress for seven years.

Seven years! In Kettering, of all places. (And us in Northumberland.) 'When did you even *see* each other?'

'Oh, you know,' Bill said rather sheepishly. 'We managed every now and again. She did a lot of the travelling.'

I was amazed. But, I must say, it made things so much easier. I took the house. Bill took the savings – rigs pay well – and he swanned off. He sent back the finished paperwork for both the house and the divorce in double-quick time (his Janet was a solicitor) and within weeks he was effectively out of my life. We had a phone call one or two months later. I had the strongest feeling Janet was listening. She'd called to him, waited till he'd picked up, then made such a clatter of putting down her extension that it was clear she'd lifted it again and was sitting, scarcely breathing, checking up on the level of emotion between us.

It must have been a very reassuring call. 'Bill,' I said, torturing him only a little for starters, 'I'm in real trouble and I need your help.'

Could a man sound more wary? 'What's the matter, Tilly?'

Off I went with my problem: a real one, all about fits and starts in the pressure chain, and problems with the new QXII valve, and knock-on disasters. Bill did a pretty poor job of hiding his relief, but he was helpful, remembering exactly what Tom (who'd retired and vanished) had always said would prove the trouble with the QXII, and suggesting a good way of getting round the problem.

Then he said, 'Hang on, Tilly. Just a minute,' and he was silent, breathing heavily. (I don't know what *she* thought.) After that, he was off again. 'No, Tilly. I'm completely wrong. Try tackling it from the gatehouse. Take down the pressure on the lower hose and . . .'

Brilliant! A small reminder of why we got so close in the first place. He'd solved my problem, so I made a point of not creating one for him. As soon as he'd finished I said to him, 'Bill, you're a gem! If I'd only had the sense to stick with consulting you rather than marrying you, both of us would have been a whole lot happier.'

Before he could blow it and queer the pitch between himself and the eavesdropping Janet, I hung up. 'Sorry. Got to go!'

That's how it is when you're childless. People like us can simply walk away. When it's over, it really and truly can be over.

Not like for poor Geoffrey. He might have tried to draw a veil over his big mistake, but, by God, the old fist kept punching through. Lost socks. Forgotten trysts at nursery school. Changes in payment schedules. Dates for holidays. It just went on and on.

At the start, his ex-wife was quite rude to me. I'd lift the ringing phone and say hello, and there she'd be, distant, dismissive: 'May I please talk to Geoffrey?'

The first two times, I handed him the phone, or called to him to pick up somewhere in the house. The third time, I was tougher. 'Listen, Frances,' I told her, 'this is my phone line and, as you know, my name is Tilly. So, when you ring, at least have the manners to say, "Hello, Tilly," before you ask to speak to Geoff. It'll make all the difference.'

Then I called Geoffrey and left the receiver lying on the kitchen counter.

Next time, she tried it on again. 'I need to speak to Geoff.'

I put the phone down and she rang back at once. 'Did you hang up on me?'

'Yes,' I said. 'You forgot the "Hello, Tilly" bit.' And I hung up again.

She rang a third time. 'Just give me Geoffrey, please. It's quite important.'

Here is another thing about the childless. We don't spend every hour God sends imagining urgent messages about our precious offspring coming in, unheard, from Accident and Emergency.

I pulled the phone plug out of the wall.

A few days later, Frances rang again. Things went quite well. The moment she heard my voice, she let out that little annoyed noise you make when you reach a recording. Then, with the restrained impatience with which people offer their security password for the third time in a row, she rattled off, 'Good morning, Tilly. Can I talk to Geoff, please?'

'Certainly,' I said. 'I'll get him at once.'

And that was that. From time to time, she would forget. I'd let it ride unless it happened twice in a row, in which case I'd say carelessly, 'Hello? Hello? I'm sorry, I can't hear you,' and hang up.

'What is her problem with me?' I asked Geoff. 'It's not as if I'm the other woman, after all. You've been divorced for ages.'

'It's nothing personal,' he assured me. 'She's just a woman who thinks in stereotypes. Her mother's the same.'

'And you,' I said, because he'd just come back from London with a present for each of his children. For Harry he'd bought a puzzle. It was a complicated, three-dimensional affair, tremendously clever in design. (I have to think that, since I spent a good deal of time over the following weeks trying to solve it.)

For Minna, he had bought two pretty hair slides.

'I see,' I told him. '"Man does, but woman is"?'

He didn't get it. 'Minna *likes* pretty things.'

'Minna likes presents,' I told him. 'All children do. And Minna especially likes getting presents from you. But what you give her shows her what you think of her. And pretty hair slides send a very unaffirming and sexist message.' I twisted the puzzle round one last time before reluctantly surrendering it for wrapping. 'Especially when you give a teaser as fiendish as that to your boy.'

I never expected something like that to lead to a quarrel. (It was our first.) He had the nerve to *argue*. I pointed out that what I'd said was no more than the truth. He still kept at it, wittering on about how Minna actually *collected* pretty things, and liked doing stuff with her hair. 'That's not the point,' I kept telling him. 'She could like licking poisonous toads, but you wouldn't offer her one as a present.'

I can't believe how long I kept trying. 'It would be fine,' I tried to explain, 'if you'd bought Harry something equally pretty and pointless.'

'Like *what?*' he crowed, as if the fact he couldn't think of anything equally vapid to give a boy proved his point, not mine. When I pointed this out, he fell in a giant sulk (manifesting itself as a hoity-toity claim to have 'far too much work to do to spend any more time on this futile discussion').

I should have ended things right then. I look back now and realize that was the moment. That was the first step down the slippery slope of mere accommodation, whereby a pair of rolling eyes foretells the death rattle. He might as well have cut the crap and come straight out with that grim marital hostility, 'Well, if you say so, dear!' At least then I would have had the sense to go after him with a pipe wrench. 'Discuss this properly, or leave right now!'

No, it is all my fault. I take the blame. I should never have let all the pleasant and easy things about living with Geoffrey outweigh the fact that right from the start we were incapable of coming to a shared understanding of any single problem, however trivial, let alone make any progress on the way to a solution. I wish I'd had the sense to face the truth back then: 'This will unpeel. I'd better get out now.' But he was very nice in bed. Clean. Pleasant-smelling. Attentive. He never spoiled the mood by lapsing into lectures on thrifty asset-management, like Sol, or trying to cadge money, like Stefan. And he was wonderful when we went out, never panicking when I reached across to take my turn at picking up the bill, and brilliant at getting taxis for exactly the right time, with no rushing or waiting. So I ignored the bad signs and just kept taking pleasure in his company – shilly-shallying, my mother would have called it – until one day, before I knew it, he had rented out his flat behind him. 'Well, it seemed sensible. After all, I can't afford to leave it sitting there doing pretty well nothing for ever.'

I took up the cudgels. 'How could you *do* that? Without even *asking* me?'

'Oh, come on, Tilly!' (He was actually trying to pre-empt me by acting more put out than I was.) 'We must have discussed this a dozen times. You've always agreed that it's plain stupid to leave the place for weeks on end, and get no rent for it.'

'Maybe I have. That's not the same as saying, "Oh, yes. Go ahead. Let someone else move in and come and live here for a year."'

'It's not a year. He's signed a six-month lease.'

'That's not the point.'

'What is the point, then?'

'That you didn't ask. You didn't even phone and check!'

'You weren't here, Tilly. You were up in Aberdeen.'

'Well, there are phones.'

'This man was in a hurry. It seemed the sensible thing. I had to decide and I didn't want to bother you.'

'How thoughtful of you,' I said bitterly. (Halfway to 'If you say so.')

Geoff played the counter-move. 'All right, I'm sorry. Clearly I misunderstood. I'll phone the man right now and tell him the deal's off and I need the place back for myself.'

'That isn't what I said.'

'It's what you mean, though, isn't it?'

And, since it wasn't, I had lost the argument. Within a couple of days, it had become so official that Frances was even told about the change. And I will have to admit it worked quite well. I bought bunk beds, and painted the spare room yellow. It was a treat to go in parts of shops I'd never even seen before to buy things like novelty wallpaper borders and pillow cases sporting favourite telly characters. In a stepmotherly fit, I even lashed out on a moody-looking rocking horse that stood in the corner, reminding me of Bill, till I finally had the sense to turn it to the window.

Only my brother expressed concern at the speed things were going. 'Moved in? But Bill's side of the bed is scarcely cold!'

'Ed, Bill left *months* ago.'

'Still – to have moved in already! What about his children?'

'They've moved in too – well, you know, Wednesday tea times and alternate weekends.'

'Oh, really, Til!' And I got quite a lecture about how long it

24

used to take the two of us to come to terms with change, and how these things should be done gradually. 'Suppose it doesn't work out?' he kept saying. 'What then? Another upheaval?' And then he asked me what their mother thought.

'I don't know,' I remember saying petulantly. 'No one's invited me to meet her properly yet.'

That set Ed off again; and I must say, when I put down the phone I did feel part of something rather low and irresponsible, as if Geoff and I had simply gone ahead and done what suited us, assuming the kids didn't mind. Since they weren't there to listen, I tackled Geoff straight away on the subject – though, not wanting to queer the pitch between him and my brother before they'd even had a chance to meet, I didn't quote Ed directly. I simply asked Geoff, as though snatching the idea out of the air, 'Do you ever worry we might be moving things along too fast?'

'Why? Don't you *want* me here?'

I made an effort not to roll my eyes. 'That isn't what I *said*. I just thought things might possibly be changing a little too quickly for Harry and Minna.'

'They seem all right to me.'

He was their father, of course. But I was still reminded of one of my tutors at university pressing upon us the vital importance of never drawing conclusions from how things looked. 'Take Galileo,' he told us. 'When he said the earth moved round the sun, everyone scoffed. "Oh, come on, Galileo! You only have to *look* to see what happens. The sun moves round the earth." And what did Galileo say? "Maybe it does look like that. But what would it look like if the earth moved round the sun?"'

Exactly the same, of course.

I was in Aberdeen the following week, but on the Wednesday after that I finally got to meet Frances properly. All afternoon the staff in Geoff's printing shop had been phoning to get him to come in and explain some complicated collating job. In the end, with Mrs Mackie twiddling her thumbs on overtime, and Frances already twenty minutes late to pick up the children, Geoff had to crack. 'You stay and watch them till she hoots.'

I put on some really noisy music to stop Harry and Minna hearing the car horn. (Damned if I'd stand for being parped at in my own home.) I kept an eye on the street. It wasn't long before I saw her car pull up outside, but I heard nothing.

Progress! I thought, and kept watching.

Frances didn't budge and, for a while, neither did I. But minutes passed, and in the end I shut the door on the children, who were still prancing about noisily in the hall, and slid out of the back door and round to the short front path.

'Hello,' I said to her. 'Geoff's just this minute had to rush down to the shop to sort out some collating. But I'm Tilly.'

For all the notice she took, I might as well have been a street sign. She was rattling her keys in the ignition. 'This bloody car's gone dead. It was playing up all the way over here. I noticed the clock was funny, then the radio went, along with the indicators.' She hammered, to no purpose, on the horn. 'Now *nothing* bloody works.'

'It'll be your alternator.' I was about to break it to her that it was a tow job, when I was checked by her 'and-how-the-hell-would-you-know?' look. Then she remembered. 'Oh, yes. Geoff told me that you studied engineering.'

'Yes,' I said. 'And now I'm an engineer.'

I don't think she took my point. She was too busy fighting the starter. 'Oh, God! Now I suppose I'm going to have to sit here till they send a man.'

It was clear what Geoff meant about thinking in stereotypes. 'Well,' I advised, 'if you should find they send a woman by mistake, don't be too quick to dismiss her. She might know something.'

And I stalked off. The minute I got in the house, I felt guilty. I switched off the thumping music and told Harry and Minna, 'Your mother's out there. I think her alternator's had it.' I waited for one of them to ask, 'Is that terrible?' or 'Will they be able to fix it?' so I could get the bad news through to Frances. But Harry just snatched up his precious furry seal and his school reading book, and ran for the door, and Minna followed, trailing the little pink rucksack in which she had packed her blankie and hairbrush, and the leaf collage she'd done in nursery. I went into the kitchen to make a pot of peace-keeping tea and, when I looked out again, Harry and Minna were already in the back of the car, strapped in and waiting, and Frances had actually been rude enough to go to my next-door neighbour's house, rather than mine, to make her phone call.

I tipped the tea straight down the sink and went back to

writing the report that I'd been working on peaceably till Geoff left. Let them get on with it, I was thinking. But the little room I was using as a study had a view of the street, and after a while I noticed that Harry, at least, had had the courage to unstrap himself and open the car door again on the kerb side. I was so grateful to him for being the only one of the three not to keep treating my house as if it were giving off noxious fumes that I went down to the kitchen and cut two giant slabs of chocolate cake as a reward. I put them on a tinfoil plate inside the basket of his new two-wheeler, and pushed the bike down the path as if I'd been about to put it away in the garage, then had a sudden thought and changed direction to walk over.

Seeing me coming, Frances let down her window just a crack.

'Sure that you wouldn't like to wait inside?' I asked her pleasantly.

'No, no.' She twisted in her seat to assure the children. 'We're fine here, aren't we? They say it won't be long.'

I left the bike propped temptingly on its support strut right beside the car, and went back to my desk. Within a minute Harry was out, and riding up and down, wobbling a little as he stuffed in a mouthful of cake each time he had his back to his mother. Curious to see what he did with the second slice, I carried on watching. First, he tried tempting his sister out of the car by wheedling so loudly even I could hear. 'Minna, I *need* you. I need your help for a *trick*.'

She stayed hunched in the back seat.

Harry reached in to try to drag her out, and I watched him being told off by his mother. Then there was quite a bit of surreptitious huddling, outside the car and in. I rather think he must have scooped the second slice of cake up under his jumper and taken it over to Minna, because at one point she was shaking her head so hard her bunches swiped her face, and recoiling even further in the back seat. So Harry gave up. He climbed out of the car and took off with the bike again, up and down the pavement, stuffing in more cake, but without enthusiasm, more as if he were disposing of evidence than wanting to eat it. And then, at last, the RAC man finally arrived. I watched as he copied down her membership details and let Frances explain. But I could see from the way he started shaking his head almost at once (and from the look of irritation she flashed the house) that he'd said the word 'alternator' and really annoyed her.

Interesting, all of it. So you could say that it was really Harry taking such care to eat only on the up-rides, and Minna trying to make herself as good as invisible, that started me reading. For weeks I read nothing but stuff about children and families. And what an eye-opener it was! Small wonder my brother had been fussing. As far as I could make out from my haphazard researches, the British had to be about the worst parents on the planet, all too willing to demand from their children the lion's share of any self-discipline going, and conveniently attributing to their offspring the feelings that they had themselves: 'Oh, yes, Mandy was upset when Alan left. But since Sam came to live with us, she's been much happier.'

'No, honestly, I know the two of them used to be very fond of each other. But now I don't think Angus gives his dad much of a thought.'

It gave me the shivers to think I might be part of one of these great towering constructions of self-deception. I was quite glad to get on a schedule of work trips that took me well away during Harry and Minna's next few weekends. When we did meet, I stuck with doing my best through meal times, then leaving the three of them to it. It was quite nice to stay ahead with all my paperwork, and in brief moments of guilt I could console myself that one thing my reading had made clear was that the principal virtues of a step-parent are unfailing kindness and a level of detachment.

And I've always been brilliant – just brilliant – at detachment.

3

IT WAS A QUALITY THAT CAME IN USEFUL NOT LONG AFTERWARDS, when Frances suddenly announced she was off to Savannah. I earwigged Geoff's side of the call. 'Savannah, *Georgia*? For five *months*? What about *my* time? How will *I* see the kids?'

She must have come up with something conciliatory in the way of offers of bed and board, because Geoffrey calmed down and started pushing for details. Who was she going with? (Terence, of course, on one of his lucrative medical contracts.) Why not stay here? (Long-winded but obvious.) The call went on for hours. I'd picked up enough about the two of them to know that if Frances suddenly felt the urge to take herself and her children off as camp followers to her new (and highly ambitious) American doctor boyfriend, Geoff had a snowball's chance in hell of stopping her. And, if I'm honest, I quite liked the idea of seeing Savannah. So when he finally put down the phone, I tried to cheer him. 'It could work out well. After all, I can get leave to go out at almost any time after the inspections. And you're your own boss.'

But it didn't turn out like that. Oh, we blocked out three separate periods on the calendar, intending to go at least twice. But Geoff's biggest client booked in such a huge run of work through the first that we had to scrub that one. By the time my second chunk of booked leave came round, my mother was acting very strangely indeed, and her neighbours were worried. 'You go without me,' I told Geoff. 'It's you the children want to see, not me.' But he just countered with, 'It would be nice to go together,' and nothing was settled. (We even lost the deposits.) The third time, just as he was fixing up the flights, in came a message from Frances that she was changing her plans (trouble with Terence?) and she and the children would be home any day now.

There was a three-week gap while Frances stayed with some old friend from school. (Her house was still rented out up here, and Torquay is enchanting in September.) And by the time the children came to us again, they might have been strangers. Harry prowled round with that disquietingly watchful look you see in adverts for the NSPCC, and Minna was even more shy than before. She thawed (at least with Geoff) within a visit or two, but it must have been a month before Geoff managed to win Harry round again. The breakthrough came when he taught Harry how to do the bloodied-finger-in-the-matchbox trick. (I played my part, putting aside my unfailingly calm instincts in the face of gore to offer up a satisfactorily convincing screech.)

That night, with the three of them finally curled up together on the sofa, young Harry summoned the courage to come out with it.

'*Why* didn't you visit us in America, Dad?'

Geoff spun him over on the cushions and gnashed his teeth, making great alligator jaws with his arms. 'Because I was frightened of crocodiles!' They ended up laughing. But that night, as I was dropping my nightie over my head, I dared to say it. 'You realize he really wanted to know.'

'Know what?'

'Why you never went out to see them. Harry wanted an answer.'

'He was just asking, that's all.'

'No. If he'd just been asking, he would have said, "Why didn't you *come*?" But he said, "*Why* didn't you come?"'

'Not sure what you're trying to say, Til.'

That weasel way of trying to block discussion has always irritated me. 'Perfectly clear, I'd have thought. The first way of saying it implies it's a casual question. The second makes it pretty clear it's been an issue.'

Geoff gave me one of those 'You-are-unhinged, Tilly' headshakes.

'Don't look at me like that,' I said. 'I'm telling you something important. This business has clearly been on his mind.'

Now here's the difference. Bill would have said, 'What are you thinking, Tilly? That he thinks I don't care enough to bother? Or that his mother's been poisoning his mind against me, or something?' And we'd have discussed it like grown-ups.

I might have persuaded him that Harry's way of asking the question was significant. He might have persuaded me it wasn't. We might even have come to some agreement in the middle, whereby we made a deal to fish about a bit for further evidence before deciding which of us, if either, was closer to the truth of the matter.

And what did I get?

'Tilly, I think I probably know my own child a little better than you do.'

'Suit yourself,' I snapped. (I have a very low tolerance for being patronized.) 'It's just I think, if he were my son, I'd do him the honour of telling him the truth, not fobbing him off with some joke about crocodiles.'

'The truth is,' Geoffrey as good as snapped back, 'that I was too busy earning money to pay the bills, and helping you look after your mother.'

You can imagine how that quarrel ended. I spent the night on the sofa. And perhaps it was sharing the cushions with Dilly the Dinosaur and Barney the Beaver that put me so firmly on the children's side, and made me vow I wouldn't ever josh them out of things when they'd had the guts to ask a real question.

And I would begin by setting Harry straight on this matter of the visit.

I wasn't quite sure how you start a conversation with a child. But early that morning, while Geoff was in the bathroom singing some silly song to Minna to try to distract her as he washed her hair, I picked up the fiendish puzzle and said to

Harry, 'If you had left this here when you went off to America, I might have learned how to do it by now.'

He didn't muck about. 'You could have come and fetched it.'

We sat on the bed and I told him, 'Your father and I worked out three separate times to come and visit you. If you look at the calendar, you can still see the yellow felt pen lines we squiggled across to keep the weeks free. But the technical college sent your dad a huge load of copying, and since a shop like his only keeps going because of big orders, he felt he had to stay. He didn't want not to be able to give your mother his share of the money she needs for you.'

He sat there quietly, twisting the puzzle round and round.

'Then when it came to the next squiggled-out bit, my mother was ill. I said I'd have to stay. He should have gone to see you alone. He probably knows that now. But he was being wet. He didn't want to have to hang around near you and your mother all by himself.'

'They're divorced, you see,' Harry explained to me.

'That would be it, then,' I assured him gravely. 'And, as for the third and last time, just as we were about to buy the flights your mum rang up and told us she was coming home.'

'Really?'

'Really.'

That easy. That easy! Harry flung his arms round me and hugged me tight. Then he ran off. I stayed in the bedroom, pretending to carry on picking up toys before following him through to the kitchen to twist the calendar straight on its hook again. Harry, by then, had rushed off to join the other two, and all of them ended up playing some astonishingly noisy game that left so much water on the bathroom floor, you'd have thought we kept seals in there. Later, when Frances drew up outside as usual and did her irritating hoot, I watched poor Harry prance from one foot to the other in an agony of indecision. For the first time since they'd come back from Georgia, he couldn't work out if he wanted to pick up his rucksack and run to the car, or stay and give yet another hug to his father.

I might have helped poor Harry rid himself of lingering doubts, but it was clear that that wasn't going to change my status in the family. The following Wednesday he was back to treating me with that stand-offish sort of sideways courtesy I'd watched him use on most of his schoolfriends' mothers. Clearly the hug had been nothing personal, only a thank you. So, out of devilry, next time I had a bit of time to waste during a pump test, I wrote Harry a letter – well, sent him a picture, really. THIS IS ME, I wrote in tiny neat block capitals above a matchstick-thin figure with copper-coloured hair that fanned out like mine. All around, I drew signs.

EXIT. LEVEL FIVE EAST. FIRE HOSE BENEATH THIS. ESCAPE HATCH. THINK SAFE, ACT SAFE & BE SAFE. NO SMOKING, NO DRINKING, NO EATING. FIRST-AID BOX. OFF-RIG SUPPLY. LASHING POINT – 3 TONNES MAX.

Nobody, not even Geoff, said anything about the picture when I came home. Intrigued, I let a couple of weeks go by, then sent another. This time I persuaded Donald in the company office to use his drafting skills to draw the rig itself, top heavy on its spindly legs like a wasps' nest spilling out all over. 'Put in a storm,' I told him when I came back from speaking to the motor men, and he drew life-rafts tossing on some giant waves, with desperate men in survival suits waving, and me with my flaming hair clearly the last to dare leap from the derrick.

Still nothing. Fascinating. I hadn't realized quite how hard it was to woo a seven-year-old.

The third time, all I did was copy one of our huge electrical wall diagrams onto a thick sheet of paper. Each time I went to another deck, one of the others seemed to pick up the pen and fill in a bit of the detail, rather like hotel guests stopping to add a piece or two to a communal jigsaw.

'Why didn't you just photocopy it from the manual?' everyone kept asking.

I pointed out that something photocopied wouldn't work.

'And this will?'

'Oh, yes. Wait and see.'

And I was right. It was the weekend after the diagram arrived that Harry cracked. Geoff put him to bed and set the shower running. I knew that Harry must have known which of the two of us was in the bathroom. (I get enough of showers on the rig.) In any case, he lingered in the doorway long enough to check it was me on the sofa before sidling in.

'That map . . .' he offered.

'Diagram.'

'Diagram. Did you invent it?'

'No,' I said. 'But if I had to, and you gave me long enough, I probably could.'

There was a pause, so I took up again. 'I mean, first time around I might not get it looking quite so tidy as that one I sent you. It's not just where the cables go, you see. Part of the art is how you set it out. Like in the Tube map.'

'Tube map?'

Just at that moment, we heard the shower splutter to a stop. 'Well,' Harry said hastily, 'thank you.' And he slid out of the room before I could offer to find a map of the Underground and explain what I meant. I didn't mind. I felt that, bit by bit, at least with Harry I was making progress. To his small sister I was still a ghost. And it was hard to work out even where to start with Minna. 'She is so in their wake,' I complained to my brother whenever he asked after her. 'She never moans or complains or wants to "do something else". She just tips her head prettily to one side, and stares with big eyes, and begs her dad to put her hair in bunches. He treats her like a pet.'

'He treats you like a pet as well, and you enjoy it.'

'But I'm a grown-up. I know what I'm getting. *And* I spend four days out of every seven staring at drainage systems and kicking men's butts. This is her image of herself this man is building.'

'Talk to him. Explain the tenets of junior feminism and step back to watch the scales drop from his eyes.'

'It doesn't work. Either he doesn't grasp it, and starts getting ratty . . .'

'Or?'

I didn't want to say it, but I did. 'Or I suspect he gets a whiff of what I mean, and gets rattier even faster.'

Ed must have said it a dozen times: 'How can you live with a man if you can't *talk* to him?' But Ed was wrong. I never couldn't talk to Geoff. Geoff couldn't talk to me. Oh, he could listen. I could bang on for hours about the rigs and their problems, or what Ed and I thought we would end up having to do with Mother as her brain thing developed. I could talk about old boyfriends, things I was reading, plays I'd seen fifteen years ago. If I had started giving him the details of ancient holidays, he probably would have listened. Talking was not the problem. No, I was allowed to talk about anything – talk until dawn if I wanted – so long as the subject I chose was on my patch.

The problem came if I stepped – ever – out of line. My life was ours, it turned out. But his was his.

At first, I'd try to come at issues in his family sideways. As when, for the third week running, Minna stared at the tubs of ice-cream ranked in front of her and said, 'I don't mind. You choose.'

I shuffled them round in front of her. 'Come on, Min. Vanilla, chocolate chip or coffee? Or a bit of all three?'

'*You* decide.'

'No, *you*. You're going to eat it, so you choose.'

Already I could sense the tension rising. 'Give her vanilla, Tilly,' Geoff told me in a firmly jovial tone. 'She likes vanilla best.'

'Then she can say so.' I turned back to Minna. 'Look, sweetpea, all the tubs are full, so you can have what you want. There won't be a problem for anyone.'

Her eyes were huge and desperate, and as painful to watch

as those of poor bullocks twisting their heads to stare out from between the slats of cattle wagons.

'Just *say* one, Minna. Take a deep breath and choose a flavour. Or two. Or all three.'

'For God's sake, Tilly! Can't you let her be?'

'*Please*, Minna.'

And the tears would spill. Later, in bed, he'd hump his back away from me, furious, and I'd say pointedly into the dark, 'It isn't right, you know. A child of her age should be able to state a preference.'

'Jesus, Tilly! What is your *problem*? Minna and I don't get all that much time together. Why do you have to think of ways to try to spoil it?'

'I'm not trying to spoil anything, Geoffrey. I'm simply pointing out that it's not natural for a six-year-old to be incapable of even choosing a flavour of ice-cream.'

He'd flounce away further in the bed. 'You're mad. You know that, Tilly? You're crazy.' We would have one of those nights. I'd lie awake, planning his funeral or my escape, and in the morning he would bring me my tea and beg my pardon. 'I'm so sorry, Tilly. I didn't mean what I said. I'm sure you're right. Next time . . .'

Next time. Always next time. But in between came all the loving and the listening and tender concern. He wove a spell around me, taking the sort of interest I didn't know one person could take in another. I became his hobby. He didn't just learn useful things, like what I like to eat and how to give me pleasure. He took an interest in everything. Soon he knew the names of every man I'd ever slept with and why I liked them (or didn't any more). He picked up all the details of my family – not just about Ed and Mum, but down to the entire series of honorary 'uncles' who came after our father. And when I told him I would rather be boiled in oil than accept the invitation to my college reunion, the look on his face was of pure disappointment.

Then there was all the spoiling. That's hard to resist. I realized after a while that, each time I clocked up the irritation of not being able to sort out some petty problem that arose between the two of us, I'd be at a disadvantage because he'd invariably just finished doing something really kind and thoughtful for me. He took such care, and kept me so pampered. I woke to tea trays and came home to ironing in neat piles, a freezer filled to bursting, and even the comforting assurance that he had found a few minutes in his busy day to ring up the nursing home and check on my mother.

'Dump him,' my brother kept warning. 'The man's not natural. He's probably a serial killer, burrowing his way into your life.'

But when Ed finally flew back to Britain, the magic worked on him as well. He came to stay while I was in the middle of the inspections. By the time I got home, Ed was full of Geoff's kindness. 'Til, he was an absolute *brick*. I told him you'd warned me all about Mum's dribbling and shouting and so forth. But he insisted he had to drive in that direction anyhow, to pick up some gubbins for one of his copiers. I'm sure that was just because he knew how shocked I'd be. And he was right. I couldn't have driven home. My hands were shaking. Literally *shaking*. He had some whisky in the car. Can you imagine? Even thought of that. The man's a marvel, Til. You make sure you hang on to him. He's bloody perfect!'

That night, just as we started canoodling, I asked Geoff, 'Don't you ever get fed up with caring for other people?'

He opened his eyes again and looked at me as if I were mad. 'What do you mean?'

'You know. All this *nurturing*.'

'Maybe it comes from being sent away to school,' he said. 'Roomfuls of bony boys for years and years. Now I just have to see a warm pink body in my bed, and all I want to do is . . .'

His voice trailed off, his hands trailed up, and that was the end of that conversation.

4

IF YOU HAD ASKED ME, WHAT I WOULD HAVE SAID IS THAT I always knew it couldn't last. It was as if this man had come along and tempted me to close a door on how things truly are, and yet inside – pretty well just at the back of my mind, not even deep down – there was always the knowledge that one day I'd have to break back through to real life waiting on the other side.

From time to time, the door would open of its own accord. Once, for example, I came back to find Geoff idly stirring onions in a pan, absorbed in a play on the radio.

'Where are the kids?'

'Oh, mooching about.'

Apart from the radio, the house seemed remarkably quiet. 'Where? Upstairs?'

'No. Outside somewhere.'

'On the street? I didn't see them.'

'They're up and down. They're playing "Tell Aunt Betsy".'

'I didn't see them,' I told Geoff again.

'I expect they're round the corner.'

I knew he was trying to hang on to the thread of what he was listening to, but I was anxious. 'What, on the estate?'

He laid the spoon against the edge of the pan and said, as if I were some four-year-old pestering, 'Tilly, what is your problem?'

'This is my problem,' I told him: 'your kids are out there in the dark around the end block of a none-too-savoury housing estate, and you're not bothered.'

'Kids need a bit of freedom. We played outside in the evenings all the time.'

'Thirty-five years ago! Things were a whole lot different.'

'This isn't Moss Side,' he defended himself; but nonetheless I saw the quite unconscious move his hand made towards the volume knob on the radio. It was quite clear he'd guessed what would be coming next: a dressing down about his parenting skills; perhaps a reminder of the most recent child to disappear off a street and be found in a ditch five days later; maybe even a slighting, 'I don't know what Frances would think.'

But what I also saw was that small furtive look of tiredness that crossed his face – that fleeting 'here we go; it's starting' expression.

I'll only have my moods predicted when I choose. Inside, I told myself, 'Not my kids. Not my problem,' and outwardly I shrugged. 'Might not be Moss Side, but it's not Toytown, either.'

On the way up the stairs, I found myself muttering, 'And

you're not bloody Noddy!' which was ungrateful since this sort of idiot optimism was at the root of Geoffrey's charm. Never seeing the bad, never fearing the worst, he was the most soothing companion. Put on ten pounds, and he'd just mutter, 'More for me to cuddle,' and hold you closer. Wear some fright of a frock and, to him, you were still the loveliest woman in the room. Living with Geoffrey was like living in Happy Valley. And, over time, the showers of stardust around him infected my eyes too. I stopped wanting to tell him, 'Listen, I'm not like you. Even since you moved in, I've slept with four separate men in Aberdeen. Last week I saw the perfect shirt for your birthday in a shop window, and couldn't be arsed to hang around for even four minutes until the place opened. And sometimes, when you ring, I shake my head at the person holding out the phone, to make them tell you they can't find me. That is the person I am. You cannot love me.'

Inside I still knew that was who I am. But with Geoff never openly admitting to seeing my faults, it gradually became easier and easier for me to forget I had any. He loved me through a haze of make-believe and, coming home to steaming casseroles, warmed sheets and theatre tickets on the mantel-piece, I was seduced along with him into living the lie. Instead of having the sense to force him into seeing who I really am, I told myself that this was natural: everyone fools themselves about love and the lover.

But truth is bedrock. You can't live for long without the truth. And, slowly, slowly, I began to see the clouds of sparkling, soothing delusions served yet another purpose. Whenever it suited Geoffrey, that gentle, shimmering miasma could be transformed into a fog of lies.

Take the weekend that Harry slid in the house like a thief, and stood around tensely. I noticed he took nothing from his schoolbag, as if at any moment he might choose to snatch it up and flee. The poor child couldn't settle all through tea. He seemed consumed with unease.

I asked him twice if he was feeling all right, then left him to it. He stayed well away from me until a phone call came to say one of the copiers had blown again. Anyone listening would have been able to track the course of the call, so by the time Geoff said, 'Give me five minutes, Doris,' Minna was already racing around the house, looking for her little pink rucksack.

'Coming?' Geoff asked her.

Minna rushed over. She adored the printing shop and all its wonders. Inside that rucksack she always seemed to have a host of drawings or cut-outs she wanted making smaller or bigger, or copying onto pink paper for her friends.

Harry hung back. 'I'm all right. I want to stay here and watch something on telly.'

'What?' I confronted him as soon as the door had closed behind Geoff and Minna. 'What do you want to watch on telly?'

He pawed the carpet.

'Come up to my study,' I said to him. 'Come up and tell me all about your interesting week.'

He scowled. 'I didn't have one.' But he did trail me up the

stairs, to lurk in the doorway, banging the drawers of my filing cabinet in and out.

'Don't do that, please.'

He knocked it off, but stayed, so I knew he was on the verge of cracking.

'So,' I said. 'All week, in school, at home, no one did anything interesting?'

A sullen, 'No.'

'And no one said anything anyone would bother to remember?'

The child was writhing. That was it, then.

'Well, come over here,' I said, 'because I have something to show you.'

It was an ancient wiring plan I'd found, inked onto grey-blue canvas so old that all the folds had cracked.

'What is it?'

'An early telephone system. One of my grandfathers was a post-office engineer.'

'Post office is letters.'

'It used to be telephones as well.'

'Did it?' He looked excited, as if he were already thinking of someone at school over whom he might triumph with this information. Then his face tensed again. I said, 'Why don't you tell me what you heard that's worrying you?'

He was back to pawing the carpet. 'Because it's rude.'

'About you?'

'No.'

'About me?'

He traced a finger round the wiring diagram. 'Go on,' I told him. 'Be a brave soldier. Spit it out. You'll feel much better.' And out it came in a fierce rush: 'She called you a canoeing bitch!'

Good thing he had the prettiest stubby fingers, and smelt of soap, or I might have snapped back, 'It takes one to know one.' Instead, I raised an eyebrow and said, 'Canoeing?'

The word 'bitch' safely out, and – in so far as he could tell – totally ignored, he was a different child. I actually sensed him relax. He reached across to run the end of his finger up and down a temptingly elegant coil design on the wiring plan, and let his soft chubby body lean against mine. 'It wasn't canoeing,' he admitted after a moment. 'It was more like ivy.'

'Ivy?'

Relief made him irritable, 'Yes. Like *ivy*.'

I changed the subject. 'Was it anything in particular, do you think, that so annoyed her?'

If he had noticed that I hadn't bothered to ask who we were talking about, he didn't show it. 'It was about not swapping over for her birthday weekend.'

'Oh, right,' I said. And since that meant nothing to me, I thought I'd better leave things there. 'Do you know,' I told him by way of an amiable wrap-up of the conversation, 'now that I think about it, I don't believe I've been in a canoe since I left school.'

And that was that. He offered to sharpen my pencils and we worked in a busy and companionable silence till Geoff and

Minna got back. That night, in the bath, it suddenly came to me. Canoeing . . . ? Ivy . . . ? Of course! Conniving! And about some birthday weekend I hadn't even known about. I wasn't going to bring it up till they were gone. (I knew there would be trouble.) And I left well before the children, on Sunday morning. But early that evening I rang from the hotel in Aberdeen. 'Have they gone home?'

Geoff sounded cheerful. 'Yup. Just back from dropping them off.'

'Geoff, when is Frances's birthday?'

There was the tiniest 'now-what's-coming?' pause before he answered idiotically, 'Not sure I remember.'

'I expect you do.'

'Of course! Silly of me. It was this month, in fact. Yes, now I think about it, it must have been a couple of weeks ago. The seventeenth.'

Don't think I didn't have my diary open and ready in front of me. 'Exactly two weeks ago, then. The weekend before last.'

'I suppose so.'

'When I was home.'

'Yes.'

'Didn't she want to swap?'

'Who?'

'Frances.'

Oh, you could tell that he was toiling. 'Swap? Swap what?'

'Weekends, Geoff. What with the Saturday being her birthday, you would have thought that she might have preferred to spend that weekend with the children.'

'Well, she had Terence.'

It was the first I'd heard that Terence was back in town again. But I was not prepared to be derailed. 'I'm right, then? You did have a little chat, and she did want to swap?'

Give him his due, he steered well clear of shifty and took quite a high tone. 'She may have hinted at it. I really can't remember.'

I, on the other hand, was not even trying to mask my sarcasm. 'Well, can you, at the very least, remember what you said to her?'

'When?'

'When she hinted at swapping weekends. What did you tell her?'

'Not sure I told her anything.'

'You didn't mention me?'

'Why should I do that?'

'I don't know, Geoff. You tell me.'

I made my voice so icy, perhaps he thought that Frances had been in touch directly to complain of my selfishness. In any event, he faltered. 'I may have mentioned that it was one of the weekends you'd be home.'

'So?'

'What do you mean, "So"?'

'Well, there are plenty of weekends I'm home. Sometimes the children are with us. Sometimes they're not. It's not an issue for me.'

'I never said it was.'

'But, Geoff, you clearly managed to leave Frances with the impression that I was the one who didn't want a swap.'

Now he was back to sounding lofty about idiot women. 'She must have misunderstood something I said.'

'Ah! So you did say something!'

'No. I just . . .'

'What, Geoff?'

'Nothing. I can't remember.'

'Was there *one single sentence* that had my name in it, along with something about not wanting a swap?'

Trapped, he lashed out. 'I thought you *liked* my children.'

I slammed down the phone. I swear that, in that moment, I absolutely hated him. I didn't sleep for plotting to get him out of my house and out of my life. At the end of my three-day stint, I was still feeling so angry that, back on the mainland, I told Donald to send the message that it had been too stormy for the chopper to pick me up.

Donald peered over his glasses. 'Tilly, how can I tell him that? The man only has to glance at a weather map to see we're as still as a millpond.'

'Then tell him we're in the middle of a blow-out, and he's to clear the line for the emergency services.'

'Oh, very funny.'

But by then, everyone in the dock office was ready to leave. I cadged a lift back to my car, and just kept driving, past home, past Newcastle, and down as far as some godforsaken strip of coastline I'd never seen before but recognized from the name as a bay of such outstanding natural beauty that we had not been permitted to put a single construction on the shoreline to support the rig, out of sight over the horizon.

It was dark and I was hungry. Following a makeshift sign, I found a tiny hotel. Over my steak pie and wine, I read the headlines in the local paper. MORE CLIFF FALLS ON FOLLY EDGE and SHEEP FOUND SAFE IN NEIGHBOUR'S FIELD. 'So not much happens round here,' I said to the barman. He seemed a little put out, and started boasting of a double suicide off Folly Leap only the month before. Not being in the most receptive mood for tales of blighted love, I fetched my jacket and went outside, hoping to walk off the resentment curdling inside me. I felt I'd been enticed by Geoffrey into having emotions I didn't choose to manage, the same way that I would hate being bullied into wearing clothes I don't feel suit me. After all, I never wanted children. So why should I have to put up with all the messiness that clings after a parting? I wanted to shriek at Geoffrey and Frances, 'Look, they're your bloody kids, not mine. So leave me out of all your petty squabbling. I have a life already. I am *busy*.'

Lord knows how long I stomped along in my foul temper. I do remember ignoring a couple of signs, and climbing a couple of fences. But I was still amazed when the dirt track beneath my feet crumbled to practically nothing, and the only thing before me was moonlight and stars.

And the cliff edge.

The drop, when I looked, must have been fifty metres or more, and I'd almost walked over. I stepped back, exhilarated. You know the feeling. It's as if the world is speaking. 'Look at me!' it says. 'I'm huge. I am astonishing. And you will never understand. So why stew in your little human irritations? Stop spoiling everything for yourself and everyone else. Be bigger. Think larger. Just get on and *live*.'

So I just sat, knees tucked under my chin, with the seat of my jeans getting colder and damper. Above, stars winked and the huge moon weaved in and out of clouds. Everything seemed to be there to transport me. Even the waves below seemed to have slowed to the rhythm of my breathing.

I can't imagine any time or place on earth more likely to settle my feelings and make me feel that things would work out well. I think I might even have driven home to Geoff that night if, back in the room, there hadn't been, in the bookcase, a thriller all the men on the rig clearly thought brilliant and talked about often. The open fire in the bar downstairs was cosy and tempting. So in the end the weekend passed, not quite the way I'd planned, in taking stock and working out how to part, but certainly in sitting alone, enjoying the solitary pleasures of reading and eating, and from time to time studying the old framed map on the bar wall, to find new walks.

On Sunday night, I finished my second book – some ancient novel I'd found tucked away on a bookshelf – and studied the slip of paper that had been lying inside and used as a bookmark. It was a guide to the location, opening hours and prices of a local attraction. 'So where's this Lartington Tower, then?' I asked the barman. 'I've walked that way at least twice and never noticed it.'

He peered at the tattered yellowing sheet I'd pushed towards him. 'Lartington Tower? Oh, that's long gone.'

'Gone?'

He made a gesture with his hand. 'Over the edge.' From under the dimpled bar he fetched out a small facsimile of the map on the wall, and, with his pen, sliced a line across a part of the coastline. 'All this has already fallen in.' He stretched his hand out flat. 'It's Britain, see? It's tilting. Over in Wales you have castles that used to be by the sea and now are stuck way out in fields, and here on our side bits keep dropping off.'

He glanced at the clock. It was eleven thirty. 'Speaking of dropping off . . .'

I took the hint, gathering up all my stuff because I was leaving so early in the morning. When I got back to Aberdeen, there was a letter waiting. It was in Geoff's large ragged handwriting and it began, *Sweetheart, from the moment you walked out of the door I have been thinking, and I have come to see that what I did was unforgivable.* It went on for three pages.

I said to Donald, 'How did he know to send it here?'

'For God's sake, Tilly. Can't you forgive the poor bastard?'

But I already had. The next four days seemed like a punishment posting, and, when I got home again, it was candles and fine wine and a hot-water bottle in the bed. 'Promise,' I said, 'that you will never, ever again dump even the tiniest smidgeon of the crap between you and Frances onto my head.'

He didn't simply promise. He dropped on his knees and took my hands in his and kissed them, and swore he'd never, ever play that trick again.

No. It was always a new one. When I was young, there were girls like that in the playground. They'd torture you with subtle variations. 'You can play nurses with us tomorrow,' they'd tell you. Next morning, thrilled and hopeful, you'd be at the school gates half an hour early. They'd show up arm in arm, wreathed in their mean little smiles. 'We said we'd let you play *nurses*. But we're playing *explorers* this morning.' On and on.

And I was never sure if Geoffrey even realized what he was doing. 'Please,' I would beg him. 'Don't tell the children you're not eating supper with them because I'm getting home late. I can eat on the plane.' 'Please, Geoff, don't pin the fact that you've not taken them to the fair on my daft schedule. You can go without me.' 'I hope you've not left Frances with the impression you can't fix the children's dates till you know mine.'

'It's a pathology,' I complained to my brother. 'I live with a man who simply refuses to take responsibility for any decision, however trivial. It always has to sound as if it's for the benefit of someone else.'

'He just doesn't want it to be his fault if things go wrong.'

'But it's so *babyish*.' I did a childish wail.' " It's not for *meeeee!*" Do you know, last time he came home with his hair cut too short, he even claimed he'd only let the barber go at it like that in the first place because he'd seen me looking at the tendrils hanging over his ears.'

'Smart thinking. If he comes out looking like a prison convict, then you're to blame.'

But that was what was so strange. Geoff wasn't into blame. I am. I go round tossing accusations out left, right and centre.

'You left the milk out all night.' 'You forgot to pick up the tickets.' 'You left Minna's bike where you might have known I'd trip over it.' But Geoff was far more generous-spirited. I could forget to lock the door behind me when I came up late at night, and he'd say nothing. I'd promise to bring home some vital ingredient for a special supper, and show up without it. One night, I even forgot that Frances had left a message about her own father being rushed to hospital with a coronary. You can imagine the stick Geoff got for not phoning back about that. And *still* he didn't bollock me.

'Mr Perfect', Ed and I used to call him, and took to playing a sort of game. I'd ring Ed any time I had a new one. 'Do you know what he said last night? "Tilly, I was brought up never to touch a banister."'

'Three points!'

We'd fall about. But in a way it wasn't funny, because it gradually became obvious that I, too, had been swept up in this extraordinary compulsion of Geoff's never to make waves. The first time I realized it was happening was when I offered to drive by the school to pick up Minna after a swimming lesson. She was easy enough to spot, one of a row of little girls doing handstands along the wall beside their bright school bags. A second bus drew up just as I took the last parking space, and since I was trapped till it pulled away again I stayed in the car, watching the kids spill off.

Thump, thump! Thump, thump! A gang of boys were swinging bags around their heads like lariats, then bashing anyone in reach. Thump! Thump! Most of the children appeared to be keeping their blows within the bounds of a game, but quite a few were being downright vicious.

I got out of the car and spoke to the bus driver. 'Aren't you going to stop it?'

He stared at me as if I'd fallen from the moon. 'They're always like this. Both ends of the ride. It's what they do to pass the time, waiting.'

'Oh, is it?'

I called the worst of the offenders to heel, put Minna in the car, then, without even thinking about it, went into the school and told the woman on reception I wanted to speak to the head teacher.

Nervously, she glanced at a woman walking past. I swung around. 'Are you the head?'

I told Mrs Dee exactly what I thought. I said if any child of mine were being thumped like that, I'd take the matter further. I said I hoped she'd get the matter sorted out, with proper supervision at both ends of the journey. (I may even have hinted I'd make a point of stopping by to check.) Then I went back to the car and we drove home. Harry was jumping about, wild with excitement at having won some special part in his class play. We all went out for supper, and the whole business slid from mind.

The call from Frances came during the week. I heard Geoff's voice rising defensively in the next room, but I had no idea the quarrel was to do with me till the next day, when a discussion about whether or not Frances would want a clump of my thinned-out lavender ended with Geoff muttering something along the lines of 'Perhaps in the circumstances it's not really the moment.'

'Sorry?' I looked up from my trowelling. 'Am I missing something? Is there some problem with Frances?'

'Not really, no.'

'No? Or not really?'

'Well, you know.'

'No. I don't know.'

'Well, weren't you listening yesterday?'

'What, to your call? No. As it happens, I wasn't eavesdropping your call with Frances. I was busy getting on with my own life.'

'Oh.' He looked as if he could have kicked himself. 'Well, it's just that she's the tiniest bit sore with you at the moment.'

'With me? But I assumed you were just squabbling about the children's dates and times, as usual. So what was it all about?'

It took some winkling out, I can tell you. But in the end I managed to piece together Frances' side of the call. The tell-tale phrases gradually stacked up: 'take it upon herself', 'interfering', 'knows next to nothing about children', 'embarrassing Minna', 'alienating the school' and, most particularly, of course, 'mind her own business in future'.

Each time I prised out a nugget, I'd find some different way of asking him 'So what did you say to that?' I can't remember a single one of his slippery, back-pedalling responses. But all of them were definitely along the lines of 'I promise I'll have a little word with Tilly.'

'Can I please get this straight?' I ended up saying. 'You and your former wife have had a conversation about my limits of responsibility. She thinks I take too much upon myself.'

'It wasn't *like* that, Tilly.'

'Well, how was it? I need to know, don't I?' I affected innocence. 'I mean, I presume the two of you still find it accept-able for me to look after your children when she's late picking them up and you have to rush down the printing shop—'

'Look, please don't think that either Frances or I is anything other than truly grateful whenever—'

'But if, for example, I were to turn up at the school and find someone threatening Minna with, say, the sharp end of a com-pass, I'm not to – what was it? – "take it upon myself" to "interfere", because I "know nothing about children". Have I got that right?'

'Now you're just being silly.'

'Oh! So I misunderstood. I *am* allowed to make my own decisions about what's safe and what's not.'

'If you could just bear in mind—'

'Of course! Minna's embarrassment! The possible alienation of the school staff!'

He'd had enough now. He was making for the door. I called out after him, 'But I can still chauffeur Minna around, I hope, for your convenience? That's still all right, I take it?'

Safe out of the room, he could pretend he hadn't heard that. Or what I called out after.

'Well, fuck your ex-wife. And fuck you!'

It was the sheer disloyalty that got to me most. As if my

house were good enough for us to live in, but I were some hired help who could be taken on for this particular morning or that rather busy afternoon, and dropped off when the job was done. I felt insulted. That night, I clawed back all the ground I'd lost the first time we'd quarrelled and I had been the one to end up on the sofa. At supper time I gave him the frigid 'no, I'm not hungry, thanks' routine, and stayed at my desk. At least three times he must have come to hover by my shoulder. 'Tilly . . .'

'Excuse me,' I said each time with icy courtesy. 'I must just finish this. I won't be long.'

I sat there, rooting further and further down the pile of stupid things to do until I realized I was checking specifications passed two weeks before. So I just read the paper until the football he was watching on telly reached a crescendo. During the action replay, I whipped into the bathroom. There, I kept up a steady clattering as I ran water into the tub, knowing he'd judge it best not to knock until I was settled. I never offered him the chance. I slid into the water while the taps were still running, and out again almost at once, so even before he realized what was happening, I was back in the bedroom, and his pyjamas were in a heap outside the door.

I don't know if I really thought he'd take it lying down. I heard the footsteps, then his knuckles rapping. 'Tilly? Tilly, open the door, please. Don't you think we ought to talk?'

He kept it up so long I felt I had to answer.

'No, honestly,' I chirruped. 'Just so long as you're still talking everything over with Frances, that's all that matters. Don't you worry about me.'

'Tilly, this is ridiculous.'

'*I'll* decide what's ridiculous. And, believe me, the one thing that'll come top of the list of ridiculous things from now on is giving a damn about you or your children.'

'Look, I know I was tactless—'

'*Tactless?*'

'And seemed ungrateful.'

'*Seemed?*'

'But, honestly, Tilly, I truly didn't mean you to be so upset.'

'I'm sure you didn't. I'm sure you would have very much preferred I'd had some sort of silent and invisible lobotomy, and was happy to fit in with whatever you and Frances decide between you is most suitable, without having any feelings of my own.'

Men hate it when you hit home. 'If you're so keen on having feelings, Til, don't forget that there's one you could try having a little more often.'

'Oh, yes? And what's that?'

'A bit of gratitude I don't share your bad temper.'

'Oh, well,' I told him. 'There you go. Nobody's perfect.'

5

STRANGE THINGS RESULT FROM ANGER. WITHIN A DAY OR SO OF acting cold indifference, I truly think that I began to feel it. Families are creepy things, and other people's families are even creepier. So, if I'm honest, it was something of a relief to be, not just given permission, but as good as ordered to stay out of the Andersons' hair. And the following week, something else happened to turn what might have proved a passing sulk into a settled frame of mind.

It was a dark grey afternoon, with icy spitting rain. Geoff thundered up the stairs. 'Tilly! Come down and look at this! It's *amazing*!'

It was a parrot perched on the tree opposite, jaunty with colour. I watched for a minute or two, sure it would fly off again almost at once, then went to find the binoculars in the back cupboard.

'Is it still there?'

'Yes. Still here. Look at that greeny blue streak all along

its belly! It's as bright as that coloured foil wrapping when you toss it on the fire.'

We stood, his arm round my shoulder, passing the binoculars from one to the other. It just so happened I was the one holding them when Frances's car drew up outside. In turn, the children leaned forward to kiss their mother before scrambling out. I lowered the glasses in case Frances glanced towards the house and took offence at being watched so closely. Harry and Minna rushed up the path to greet their father. We had a perfectly pleasant afternoon. I raised the topic only over supper.

'Did your mum notice the parrot?' I asked Minna.

As usual Geoff didn't give her space to answer 'You didn't even know it was there till I pointed it out, did you, Minna?'

'Oh,' I said. 'I thought your mother might have stopped the car a little way up the street, to watch it.'

Both children were staring. 'No.'

'Oh, right,' I said. 'It's just that neither of you was wearing a seat belt when you arrived.'

Minna stayed silent, of course. But Harry thought he was on solid ground. 'Oh, no. That wasn't the parrot. That's because all the strap buckles are stuck under.'

'Under the seat? Doesn't your mother worry?'

He made a 'never-really-thought-about-it' face, though I could tell from Geoff's uneasy shifting that he, at least, was sniffing trouble. But I kept on. 'It's a real nuisance, of course, putting those sorts of back seats up and down. The strap buckles always seem to vanish. What were you carrying, anyway?'

'The Christmas tree,' Minna remembered. 'You can still get needles in your legs.'

'Prickly!' I sympathized (though I meant 'Bingo!'). I changed the subject. Geoff's unease melted away, probably before he even realized he was feeling it. And only when the children were safely gone that evening did I open fire.

'It's January the twelfth,' I reminded Geoffrey. 'If Frances had her tree up by Christmas Eve—'

He wasn't thinking. 'Christmas Eve? You must be joking. Frances is so bloody organized her tree is always up well before that.'

'Say the eighteenth, then. That makes five weeks, at least.'

'Five weeks of what?'

'Of Harry and Minna not wearing safety belts in the car.'

There was such silence, I felt sorry for him. There he'd been, offering me a friendly nugget about his former wife, and, in return, what had I given him? Any way you look at it, trouble.

'I'll dig the straps out for her next time she comes.'

'She's driving the children down to York tomorrow.'

'I'll give her a ring.'

'Now?'

'In the morning.'

'But you don't know what time she's leaving.'

'Then I'll ring early.'

'Maybe you ought to ring her now.'

'Tilly . . .'

'Geoff?'

He was looking at me strangely, and seeking something in my face. I turned away, ostensibly to get a fresh drying-up cloth from the drawer, but really to stop him trying to work out what was fuelling my relentless pursuit. His own suspicions sparked off mine. Was it, I asked myself, truly what I'd have answered if he had challenged me? That my entire career revolved around matters like these. The safety standards of over a hundred oilmen lay pretty well in my hands. I'd watched more safety videos than I'd seen washing-powder adverts, and knew the exact force of bodies hurling through the air. Of course I wasn't going to say, 'Well, you know best, dear. They're your children,' and let the two of them get on with their sloppy and dangerous habits.

Or was it, at root, nothing to do with Harry and Minna? Something a little darker? Perhaps some predatory desire, born of sheer irritation, to hound the man who had so recently humiliated me on this same issue of the welfare of children. Perhaps I was simply getting my revenge – taking advantage of the situation to stamp on the shadows behind him and keep him on the run. Because Geoffrey never did make the effort to ring Frances. And I didn't make him because I didn't really care. It must be the worst thing on earth to grow to love a child yet have no say in things that happen to it. Either you would go mad with anxiety or you'd bail out. And on that evening after the parrot came, I had to face a quite unpalatable fact about myself. One little setback had stopped me bothering. I look back now and see my only real purpose was to set Geoffrey squirming so I could better see how he unravelled, in exactly the same way I'd try to understand a piece of machinery by taking it apart.

And so that wrangle came, like every other, not to a proper conclusion, but to an end. Yet most of the time we were still perfectly happy. That summer, Ed came home to help me move our mother yet again as her condition worsened, but I remember it as one long pleasant time. Poor Mum's relief at no longer being 'strongly encouraged' to get out of bed each day was plain from the start. Her brain worked no better in the new place; but, no longer baffled by handles and switches and taps, she clearly felt warmer and safer, and her fantasies became less fearful. I started coming home from the nursing home in perfectly good spirits.

'Good visit?'

'Went a treat.'

'So who did she think you were today? Good or Bad Tilly?'

'It's not quite as simple as that,' I told him wryly. 'Even within an afternoon it shifts about. Today I even wondered if it might depend on something as simple as where I happen to be sitting. I mean, she did ask, "Where's that other one? You know, the one with hair like yours who sits reading the paper by the window?" But when I said, "Mum, that one's me as well. It's just that sometimes I sit over there because the light's better," she just let it go — except to say she hoped the other one didn't come back till after I'd gone.'

'Why's that?'

I burst out laughing. 'Because she's rather stand-offish, apparently. And Mum says she much prefers *me*.'

Geoff pulled the cork out of the celebratory bottle of wine that signalled Duty Done. 'So what do you reckon, Tilly? Has she settled enough to be left for a whole month? Is France on or off?'

And France was on. When I looked back, I realized that I hadn't had a proper holiday in as long as I could remember. And Geoffrey did it all. He fixed up a lovely rented cottage in an apricot orchard. There was a tiny shaded pool. Cows stared at us over the hedges. And everywhere we walked, we saw signs warning us of bulls. I felt my bones melt as days drifted past. I didn't notice what we talked about, and, in that heat, all conversations were desultory.

It was a magic, magic time. I'd look at Geoffrey, looking down at me with real desire, and think myself so lucky. He'd put his arm around me as I picked my way in high heels down the rutted path on the nights we went out to smart restaurants. He peeled me oranges, and skimmed the dead bugs off the surface of the pool before I swam. And I have never in my whole life thought, I'd love these days to last for ever, as I did then.

Then we drove back to the ferry. Even the crossing seemed to be part of the holiday. It was only as the car tyres rolled over the noisy metal sheeting between the boat and the quayside that Geoffrey showed his first doubt. 'We could just skip this visit. He doesn't know we're coming. We could just shoot up to the motorway straight away, and miss the traffic.'

'Geoff, he's your *father*.'

'We'll simply pop in, then. Just for a cup of tea, that's all.

We'll make it clear right from the start that we're not staying.'

I was intrigued. Did he suppose his dad was going to *hate* me? Geoffrey kept glancing at his watch. 'What's the problem?' I asked him. 'Even if we don't get as far as home tonight, it doesn't matter.'

'It's not that.'

'What is it, then? You keep on checking the time.'

'No, I don't.'

'Geoff,' I said. 'Stop the car.'

'Don't be daft, Tilly.'

'I mean it. Stop the car.'

He pulled up on a garage forecourt, out of the way of the pumps. 'What is the *matter*?'

'I want to know why you're looking at your watch every few seconds.'

'I'm not.'

I sat there patiently, watching the traffic flash past as if I'd be happy to sit there for ever. 'All *right*,' he said at last. 'Maybe I am. I didn't realize that I was, but maybe I am.'

'But *why*?'

It was like watching something made of mud attempt to think. He made the process appear downright painful. 'I suppose . . .'

'Yes?'

'I suppose . . .' He squirmed. 'I suppose I'm worried that, the later we get to Briar Cottage, the drunker he'll be.'

Too right! Geoff's father might not have been swaying or puking, or saying, 'See you, Jimmy!' every thirty seconds like half the drunks in Aberdeen. But he was no picnic to visit. He spent a lot of time pretending I wasn't there, and, when he did admit that I was on the planet, he wasn't pleasant. He made a face as I kicked off my sandals – honestly, you'd have thought I'd stepped out of my knickers – and glowered as I picked my way barefoot down the bank into the tiny brook that ran along the end of his garden. I paddled in a daft way, up and down, willing the moments to pass. He stared at me with utter scorn for a while, then said to Geoffrey loudly enough for me to hear, 'Is she always this idiotic? Doesn't she realize she's ruining my precious marsh marigolds?'

Mortified, I clambered out and, in a desperate attempt to prove myself more sensible than a paddling toddler, asked, 'Do you get much pollution in the stream?'

'None,' he said, 'till you stepped in.'

I couldn't help but gasp. I don't believe that, since I left primary school, anyone has ever been so rude. I would have thought that I'd misheard, if he'd not followed it up as we were leaving. Staring down at the car as I was climbing in, he said to Geoffrey, 'What's that on the back seat?'

Geoff glanced at the unopened packet of batteries lying there, waiting to go back to the shop to be exchanged for ones the next size up. 'Oh, that's just one of my mistakes.'

In the wing mirror, I saw his father's thumb jerk my way and, with the car windows open, heard him say it clearly enough. 'You mark my words, boy. So is she.'

We must have driven for at least a mile with neither of us saying anything. I could only suppose Geoff was waiting for some explosion. But what did it matter to me? Geoff had as good as warned me. And, after all, it's not as if I were eighteen and dying to be part of a brand-new family, or planning to have children who might want to paddle in the stream in their turn, and call the grumpy old fart 'Grandpa'. So after a while I said, quite fascinated by the whole grisly experience, 'Do you know, I do believe your father is the rudest man I've ever met.'

Geoff's fingers tightened round the steering wheel. 'Well, he was *drunk*. I did warn you.'

'Yes,' I agreed. 'You did warn me. And a good thing too, since he is almost unbelievably offensive.'

That's when he said it. 'Tilly, he is my *father*.'

People who use cloth for brains have always got on my nerves. 'Yes,' I said, 'you are right that he's your father. And I am right that he's the rudest man I've ever met. Both of these statements can be true at the same time, and both of them are.'

I don't know what made me mutter under my breath, 'Unless, of course, you were *adopted*.' But that was a step too far. Geoffrey fell in a sulk that lasted for sixty miles. I did try pulling him out of it once or twice. I twittered on about the colour of some cows in a field, as I recall. And once or twice I remarked on the number of squashed pheasants. But after a while I felt more cross than guilty. After all, what was Geoffrey doing except for closing down a conversation that was making him a shade uncomfortable? Well, he might prefer to live in his own little Noddy world in which no one – not even his father's most recent victim – had the temerity to point out that the man was rude; but I'm on the planet too, and I didn't see why I had to sit beside him in the car all the way home, forbidden to speak of what was uppermost in my mind, or talk about the visit properly. After all, it would have been *interesting*. Had Geoffrey's father's behaviour been unusual for him? Or was that always the sort of thing he dealt out to strangers? And, if it were, then when did he turn that rude? Who let him get away with it till it became a habit? Did he have any friends? I would have loved to hear Geoff's views on why his father acted the way he did.

But Geoff preferred not to think about it. And that, from his point of view, was that.

If he'd been stupid, I am sure I could have let it go. I might even have been able to bring myself – by Doncaster, say – to come out with something emollient: 'I'm sorry what I said about your dad upset you so.' (The weasel marital apology: not sorry I said it – just sorry it upset you.) But anybody who can fix a jammed photocopier must have a working brain. So I was just annoyed at Geoff's sheer stubbornness. I knew from the clipped way he brushed aside my questions on our choice of route that he was trying to make me feel like a naughty child who'd gone too far. And that led to our next argument.

'Can we change places?' I asked him after a while.

'I'm quite all right,' he said. 'I'm fine.'

'I expect you are. It's just that I would like to drive for a bit, please.'

'Tilly, we're nearly there.'

'I'd like to drive, please. Would you stop the car.' As if the very road were on my side, up popped the sign for a lay-by. 'That will be fine,' I said firmly.

'Tilly—'

'It is my car, Geoffrey.'

He'd forgotten that. And, interestingly, that is what swung the matter. He started moving towards the inside lane. In the lay-by, the two of us switched places without exchanging a single word. I know what I was doing. I was refusing to be driven a single mile further by someone who wouldn't talk to me. It's a control thing, like picking up the bill after an argument in a restaurant because you can't bear to be beholden to someone whom you've decided you don't like.

Not speaking seems a whole lot loftier when you are busy changing lanes. After ten miles or so, Geoff started talking. Not about his father. (That would have been too much of a climb-down – not to mention a topic of real interest.) About something utterly bland and forgettable, like weather or cars. But the message was definitely: end of sulk.

Still, I kept concentrating on the road. And when, as we unpacked the car, he tried to wrap up our holiday by saying something really nice, I hurried out of earshot. When he came up to bed I was already pretending to be asleep, though I was back to planning my escape. I lay there with the 'Sorry, Geoff, this isn't working' speech echoing round my brain, and ran through the pros and cons of selling the house and moving to a flat in the city. Finally I dozed, but only as lightly as I could, since I was determined to beat the alarm clock and switch it off before it woke him. In the morning, I didn't even make toast in case the smell floated up the stairs. And I was safely outside on the doorstep a full ten minutes before the taxi arrived. I was determined not to hear a single word about our future till I had had the time to tell him that we didn't have one.

I flew up to Aberdeen with every nerve end charged for parting. So I blame the North Sea. Lean with your arms stretched flat along a railing, and stare out. From a rig deck there's nothing to distract you: no strips of sand, no walkers on the beach, no rocks on which the breakers slap, and slide back down again in dark wet patterns. All that we have is waves. Great powerful, timeless, surging waves. They are mesmeric. For a few minutes or so, your brain keeps tossing up the stupid surface thoughts. 'This will be here for eternity.' 'I could stand here for ever.' 'This will go on and on when I am dead.' But after a while, you simply watch. And watch, and watch. On land, it's cold or hunger that makes you move on in the end. We're so wrapped up, we could stay warm as far north as the Arctic. And life's so dull that all we do is eat too much, then snack on chocolate. It can be noisy, depending on who's clanging about above or below. But if you choose the right spot, most of the hum of the generators blows away, and leaves you with just the wind whipping around you.

In sets that sense of being tiny in the universe. An ant. An apple pip. Something so small and unregardable you may as well not exist. You are reminded of all the aeons you weren't here, and no one knew or cared. You think of how, within a few years of your vanishing, things will be like that again. You look at all those waves and think, I am a blink in time. I go two ways. Sometimes I find it quite exhilarating. Thrilling. Inspiring. I feel as if I could go anywhere, do anything. Impatience seizes me. I want to pack in this small life and pick another. Choose to be anything. Fly!

At other times in comes the void. I get the sense that life is worthless, pointless and drab, and nothing matters. A grey fog settles and clings. Usually I'm glad to get off a rig. On days like these, it makes no difference. I go through the motions, gather my stuff together and scramble aboard as usual. But it takes time to come back to myself and feel a person, not just a walking, talking 'thing' pacing out life on the planet.

Back at the terminal, there was a message. 'Please phone Geoff.'

'I'm off home anyhow,' I lied to Donald. But he had picked up a ringing telephone. 'Oh, right. No, she's still here.'

He handed it to me.

Geoffrey.

'Hi, sweetheart. Back at the terminal, having a cup of tea with Donald before the taxi arrives?'

I looked at the mug in my hand, with steam still rising. He could, I knew, have caught me almost any time, on almost any day, and got it almost as close. If a man goes to the trouble of asking you about your day and listening to your answers – triumphs and grumbles – and cares enough to remember, then he will learn how your weeks work. I could imagine some woman who adored Geoff making a call to say much the same to him. 'Hi, Geoff. Are you busy explaining to Mrs Mackie the jobs that came in since she went off for lunch?'

Someone.

Not me.

But still, the grey mist lifted. Believe me, I so wanted us to part that I tried clinging on to it. I almost felt myself trying to hug depression round me. But sad, weird moods come and go as they choose, and this one chose to go. All I was left with was a warm and loving feeling. This man so cared for me that, all through his day, he kept me firmly in his mind. He knew where I might be, and what I might be doing. Who I was with and how long it might take. I mattered to him. So I mattered.

And suddenly, whether I could talk to him about his father mattered less.

6

IT WAS MINNA WHO FIRST MENTIONED 'MUMMY'S BUMP' ONE weekend morning. I can't remember why she came out with it, but the expression struck me at once.

'You don't suppose she's pregnant?' I whispered to Geoff as I passed him a cereal box to put back in the cupboard.

'Who?'

'Frances, of course. Weren't you listening? Minna said she has a "bump".'

Just at that moment, Harry came back in the kitchen to pick up his radio-controlled rat. Sensing that we were having a private conversation, he hung around, so it was quite a while before Geoff picked up the topic again. 'Of course she wouldn't be pregnant. Frances is far too old to start again.'

'Geoff, she's barely scraped forty! And Minna is only nine. It's perfectly possible.'

'Nonsense. Whose baby would she be having?'

'Terence's, of course.'

'But they've split up again.'

News to me. But at that moment the notion of Frances having a 'bump' intrigued me far more than the fact that Geoff evidently hadn't bothered to keep me abreast of yet another milestone in his family. 'Perhaps that's why. Maybe Terence didn't fancy being a father.'

'Tilly, you're mad.'

Not mad. Just wrong. The real facts of the matter came home to us only a couple of Wednesday visits later, when Harry dumped a bigger load of stuff than usual on the hall floor. 'Mum wants us to sleep over here, and for you to take us to school in the morning.'

'Brilliant!' said Geoffrey.

'Is there a reason?' I couldn't help asking.

Harry looked grave. 'She's seeing someone early about her lump.'

'Oh, *lump*,' I said, caught off guard. Harry gave me a look. 'I thought it was "bump",' I admitted.

'No. Lump,' said Harry. He seemed a hair's breadth away from tears. I took it he'd picked up more than just the word, so put a warning hand on Geoffrey's arm as I said cheerfully, 'It's good the two of you are sleeping over. Your dad was hoping you could stay a bit later tonight. He thought it would make a nice change to go to a film.'

We all switch moods in an instant, but only children are honest enough not to try to conceal it. 'Film?' Harry was already bouncing up and down. 'What, in town? Can we go to *Ghost Train*? Please! Everyone in my class has seen it already.'

ANNE FINE

'Is it too scary for Minna?'

We watched the struggle between longing and honesty. I let him off the hook. 'I thought, if Minna stayed here with me, I could help her bake chocolate fingers to take to school tomorrow.'

Minna looked up. 'Or fairy cakes? Like the ones you made with Harry when I had the flu?'

'Whichever you like.'

So that was settled. Harry was distracted from his worries, and Minna, busy with her wooden spoon, turned really chatty. First, I heard all about her myriad little feuds in school. Then all about her triumph at the gym club. Finally, she mentioned how cross her mother had been when the oven packed in twice in one week, and I took the chance to drop the little question. 'So where's this lump of hers, then?'

Minna let go of the mixing bowl to reach up and touch the side of her neck. I leaned across to wipe off the butter smear before it ran down to her collar. 'Is it big?'

'It's getting bigger.'

'Has she seen the doctor?'

'She's seen . . .' Minna laid down the spoon to tick them off on her fingers. 'Three doctors and two special doctors and a puncturist.'

'*Acu*puncturist?'

'Yes.' Out came the bombshell. 'And now she's going to America and we're to come and stay with you till she gets better.'

'Really?'

'Next week, when Terence has it sorted.' She reached for the egg I'd been holding out, and fell silent with concentration for the time it took to crack it in the cup and whisk it creamy. I thought I might have to prompt her, but as soon as she'd tipped the first slither of beaten egg into her batter she came back to the subject of her own accord. 'Terence's cousin is a . . .'

She stopped and stared at me with that old haunted, agonized look.

'Surgeon?'

She shook her head.

'Specialist?'

It finally came to her. 'Oncologist.'

'That's some word to remember!'

She gave me one of her rare smiles. 'Want to know how I do it? I think of pigs.' She saw my blank look. 'Oink, oink! Oinkologist!'

It seemed as good a time as any to exit the conversation. I led her off the topic by going on to chat about two of Geoffrey's own animal imitation specialities (braying like a donkey and mooing like a cow) and other matters. I knew the rest of the story would filter in when Frances rang, and it was comforting to feel that, just this once, I knew a little more than Geoffrey about what was happening in his family.

Much good it did me. Geoffrey took the call. I stayed out of sight but, this time, I was listening hard. And when he came to find me and report, it was as clear as paint that he was telling only the half of it. I offered him the chance to come clean. 'So Frances didn't give you any idea how long she'd be gone? That seems a little strange.'

He shrugged. 'I don't expect she knows. From what I gather, it's some sort of weird experimental place. You know, organic berries, yoga, imagining your red blood cells busy chewing up the cancer.'

'White blood cells,' I corrected automatically.

'Whatever. Anyhow, I got the feeling the whole idea was that she let go of all her troubles and responsibilities to give her body a clear run to get better.'

I made a face. I had no way of proving that all the assurances I'd overheard Geoff making had any relevance. (Yes, he'd make sure they had their dental inspections. No, he wouldn't forget to pay next term's gym-club fees.) But I was certainly suspicious enough to turn mean-spirited. 'Still, sending your children round to someone else's house indefinitely . . .'

'I'm not just "someone else".'

'It's not your house.'

He bridled. 'Are you suggesting I should have said no to offering a home to my own children?'

'No. I just think it would have been nicer if you had said, at some point in the call, "I can't for a moment imagine there'll be a problem. But I will of course have to check with Tilly."'

'I think I did say something like that at one point.'

'Geoff, as it happens, I was listening. And I know for a fact you didn't.'

Now he was getting ratty. 'Well, if there's no problem, why on earth should I have gone to the trouble of bothering to say it?'

It was the careless little 'bothering to' that riled me. 'Because this is *my house*. And I think you and Frances have a really bad habit of taking me too much for granted.'

'For God's sake, Tilly! The mother of my kids turns out to have cancer, and you're just on about who owns this house!'

And, put like that, it did sound very petty. But I was seething. For it did seem to me that there was always some great highfalutin reason why the two of them could act as if I didn't count for anything whenever it suited them. I didn't push the issue. Clearly it wasn't the time. And Geoff was quite sincerely upset at the news about Frances. The children moved in only a few days later, and my suspicion that they'd be staying a whole lot longer than Geoff was actually letting on was strengthened by his wistful hint that I might let him dismantle the bunk bed and move Harry's half into the room I'd always used as an office. (I turned a deaf ear.)

The children started off as usual, with that same somewhat distant 'politesse' they'd always shown under our roof. But there's a deal of difference between visiting and living, and as the days went by I saw a different side of both. Minna, for example, was still as quiet and undemanding as before, and it was the usual effort to get her to commit herself to even the smallest decision. But I began to notice that she could make her feelings clear by taking her time. I'd ask her, 'Would you like to come with me to pick up the supper?' Half an hour later the restaurant would ring. 'Is there a problem? Your order's sitting waiting,' and Minna would still be sitting on the bottom stair, taking an age to pull on a sock or button up a shoe. I'd ask her to set for lunch, and though, each time I looked round, she'd be moving obediently between the cutlery drawer and the table, still, when the meal was ready, however long that took, her job was only half done. She ate at a snail's pace. She took so long to get into her pyjamas that there was never time for a story. She never complained, never said no, never failed to agree about anything. But still she couldn't have made her feelings about staying in our house more obvious. It was like living with a child who walked through glue.

Harry, by contrast, shifted tirelessly from one room to another, a thin tuneless whistle seeping from between clenched teeth. He started every single one of the books Frances had sent along with him, and finished none. He fiddled with the controls on the radio till I could have slapped his fingers. He took to tormenting his sister. And shadows deepened round his eyes.

'Talk to him, Geoff. He's probably got it in his head his mother's dying.'

'What am I supposed to say?'

We sat in mutual bafflement. What are the words for someone whose mother feels herself to be – probably is – in such great peril that she's gone to Arizona for a 'miracle cure'?

'Tell him . . .' I hesitated. Nothing seemed right. 'Just get him talking.'

'It's not that easy, Til.'

And yet it was. Night after night I woke to hear the struts of the bunk bed creaking like a galleon at sea. I'd pad through to pull the covers back over his thrashing limbs, and end up staying till I froze while Harry kept me, clinging to company by explaining in pitiless detail why he had woken, or how he couldn't sleep.

It's not surprising that in the end I cracked. 'All *right*. Unfasten the bloody bunk bed and put his half in my study. At least that way I won't be standing half the night.'

'I'm sorry, Til.'

Not sorry enough to get the boy talking himself, of course. And how I hated what I had to listen to, because poor Harry was consumed with foul intrusive thoughts. Every black tale he'd heard at school, every warped headline he'd seen in papers, ran riot through his brain.

'So there was this murderer—'

'Who told you this one, Harry?'

'Kevin. His brother told him.'

I'd sigh. Harry would pick up the story. 'It's true, Tilly. He murdered this girl on the beach, then turned her face down with her arms stuck in the sand as if she was doing press-ups. And when the police pulled her out, they found she only had stumps.'

'Stumps?'

'The murderer had cut her hands off.'

My stomach churned. 'Christ, Harry! Who feeds you this crap?'

'Don't say "crap", Tilly. It's rude. I *told* you. It was Kevin's brother.'

'He made it up.'

'No, honestly. It really happened.'

Night after night. A merciless stream of grim stories. Crucified children. Set-on-fire dogs. Disembowelled horses. Girls chained for years in cellars. What can you find to say to comfort a child when your own heart is thumping?

I spoke to Geoffrey. 'That boy needs help.'

'Help?'

'Someone professional to talk to. His brain is swimming in this crap. He's drowning in horrors.'

'I'm sure it'll pass.'

'Why? Because that's an easier thing to think?'

'That's a bit spiteful, Tilly.'

'Hit home, did it? Maybe you should consider if there's a bit of truth to it.'

And out it came on cue, the perennial whitewashing claim: 'I think I know my own child.' With no spare bed to sulk in, I simply turned my back. But only the dead drunk and the born insomniac can share a mattress with someone they're busy despising, and after a couple of sleepless nights I made my offer. 'Let me pay for it. Let me find someone who can help him. He needn't even know it's therapy. He's only eleven, for God's sake. We can probably kid him that he's helping out with some survey, or something.'

'No, Tilly.' I saw Geoff's face brighten as a notion came to let him off the hook. 'It wouldn't be right unless I asked Frances.'

Smart way to kick that ball straight into touch. Who's going to phone a woman who is eating Mexican weeds and practising 'positive visual imagery', and tell her that her son's so frightened she's going to die that every dark thought in the world is camped in his brain?

Not even me.

I took a break from the whole boiling. First, I phoned Donald. 'Pass the word,' I said. 'Anything. Anywhere.' Within hours, the first call came in. 'Tilly? Donald says you'll trade a week on rig for time later in the year.'

'Spot on.'

'Trouble at home?'

'Just need a bit of space.'

'I'll take it! Shall I tell Luis you're in the market for the weekend as well? His wife's going through the wringer with this new baby.'

See? Easy-peasy. But when I came home, nothing was any better. In fact, things were worse. I got in far too late to see the children on the Sunday night, but when I came down in the morning it was to find Minna already in tears, barricaded behind cereal packets. 'Harry's being mean. He keeps on saying I've got such big nostrils that everyone can see up to my brain.'

'He can't help being a halfwit.'

She used her pyjama sleeve to wipe off slug trails. 'And he keeps saying my knickers smell and everyone talks about it.'

I turned to Harry. 'Out!'

She took some comforting. I held her close and patted while she hiccuped and snivelled. Gradually, out spilled the horrid things he'd said and done, and got in trouble for at school.

'They've even sent a letter.'

'Here?'

'Arif's mother *made* them. Arif told everyone. Didn't Dad tell you?'

I played it loyal, muttering something inane. 'Oh, *that* letter. I thought you meant some other letter.' But Minna's litany of her brother's sins had at least had the cheering effect of reminding her he was the one in deep trouble. Wiping her nose upward with spread palm, she now declared herself recovered enough to slip off my knee and go back up the stairs for her school bag. I sat hearing the thump of her footfalls over-head and asking myself if I could possibly have failed to register Geoff's mention of any letter from the school, and wondering if he had any intentions at all of saying anything about it in the future. Even as I was laying my psychic money on 'no', I heard the rattle of post through the letterbox and onto the mat fell a letter addressed to Mr and Mrs Anderson. Even with Minna's warning uppermost in mind, I opened it without a thought, simply assuming that, as usual with such letters, it was a special offer from a garage he had visited, or a suggestion that we switch some household bill that was under Geoff's name over to some other system of payment.

It was another letter from the school. It spoke of continuing problems with Harry and referred to more money going miss-ing, 'unlikely denials', and a further rash of tantrums and fights. It even made mention of 'Mr Anderson's visit last month to discuss matters', and suggested it was time that we set up another meeting.

I'd only been gone a week. A single week! I read the letter several times, then left it unfolded on top of Geoff's heap of post before ushering the children towards the back door. 'Come on. I'll take you this morning.'

'But Dad's nearly finishing shav—'

'No, no. It's late already. Come along.'

I know they sensed that there was trouble brewing. They clambered in the car without the usual fuss about front seats and 'turns'. Each time I glanced in the mirror, Harry's eyes caught mine, then dropped at once. Minna was scarcely breathing. The sheer relief of both when we reached the school was pretty well palpable.

' 'Bye, Tilly!'

' 'Bye, Tilly!'

I took my time driving back. (Letting Geoff stew.) But I'd be daft to think Geoff needed any help from me in postponing an argument. By the time I got home he'd vanished to the printing shop. And though I heard his key in the lock around eleven, it must have been at least an hour before he dared come up to the bedroom, where I was working on my knees in an armchair.

'About this letter, Tilly . . .'

He tossed it sideways onto the bed.

'Yes?'

'I had been meaning to tell you.'

'Tell me what?'

'What's been going on with Harry.'

Could I have sounded less convinced? 'Oh, really?'

He coloured. 'Yes, really. It's been a difficult week.'

'Longer than that, by all accounts.'

'It did start a little bit earlier, yes.'

I reached for the letter and waved it in the air. 'Judging by what's in here, it must have started a whole lot earlier than our conversation about finding Harry someone to see him through all this.'

'The thing is, Tilly, I didn't see how that would help.'

'The thing *is*, Geoff, the discussion that we had – perhaps I should say the discussion that I *tried* to have – was in entirely bad faith. I wanted to talk about your son's problems and all you were doing was hiding every single piece of information that might have led to—'

I broke off, suddenly exhausted. It seemed to me that I could see the end of every single conversation before we'd even started it. 'Listen,' I told him. 'Not giving people the facts is quite as deceitful as lying. It's simply a different way of being dishonest.' Filled with exasperation, I practically pushed him aside in my eagerness to make for the door, but, as he followed me to the top of the staircase, I made the mistake of putting the boot in. 'Oh, yes. And, of course, it is a whole lot more *craven*.'

Behind me, I heard the strangest little popping noise. I turned to look. Geoffrey had turned beet red. His fists were clenched. Framed by the narrow upstairs landing, he had the look of someone in a comic strip – one of those characters so angry that steam's coming out of their ears. And when he finally managed to get out the words, his voice had shot high as a child's. 'Oh, shut up, Tilly! You are such a fucking *moralist*!'

I stared up. He stared back down, pop-eyed in his wrath. 'Don't look at me like that, Tilly! Look at yourself. Talking to you is like having skin stripped off. Want to know why I don't tell you things? It's because I can't stand what happens the minute you get your sharp little teeth into them.'

My breath came back. 'What's that supposed to mean?'

'What do you *think*?' he shouted. 'You *feed* on other people's weaknesses. You *love* their petty failures. You know your problem, Tilly? You think you're doing something positive. "Taking an interest in people."' He was shaking with rage now. 'But what you're *really* doing is gathering little lumps of ammunition. And as soon as you've worked out just how someone close to you ticks, then you start getting your jollies punishing them with all the small cold truths about themselves. What could be sicker than that, Tilly? What could be sicker than *that?*'

I was astounded. If he had punched me, I couldn't have been more shocked. It was exactly what my mother said when I was seventeen. 'Tilly, you'll come to no good. You have an evil gift for twisting what you know about people round into knowing exactly how to upset them.'

One person might get you wrong. But two? Far more unlikely. There was a rushing in my ears and suddenly my knees gave under me. In moments Geoff was at my side. 'Oh, Tilly! Oh, God! I'm so sorry! I didn't mean what I said. I was just upset because I should have told you about the letter. Please forgive me, Tilly!'

I can still see us there – me on the edge of the hall chair with my legs still shaking; him on his knees in front of me, his arms around my waist, hugging me to him. 'Oh, Tilly! Please! Let's try again. I won't tell any more lies. I won't keep secrets. I will tell you everything. This is *ridiculous*.'

I will admit it, I felt like a murderer whose victim rises from the grave to say, 'I'm sorry. It was all my fault.' The truth stung till I couldn't breathe, but I'd have given the world for him not to realize that what he'd said hit me so hard. I think I was praying he'd be true to form, and keep on thrusting all those harsh black words of his back down into that part of him so practised at burying everything painful. I'm sure it was only because I was so desperate to distract him that I managed to summon – God knows from where – the presence of mind to lead his thoughts as far away from me as possible. 'Look, Geoff, none of this matters now. We can sort it out later. What's important is Harry and his stealing. What does he say about that?'

Bank upon one thing: the need of people like Geoff to slide away from unpalatable truths outweighs all else. Within a flash, the errant lover in our little tableau had recast himself. The caring parent frowned. 'He says it isn't true.'

Distraught as I may have been, I was still startled. 'What, none of it? Is he saying he's never stolen anything from any of the children in school?'

Geoff's distress turned to sheer embarrassment. Clearly he knew what crap he was talking before he even spilled out the words. 'He swears he hasn't, Tilly.' The chin went up.

The serious look spread over his face. 'And of course, as his father, I have no choice but to believe him.'

What utter horseshit! No two ways about it: good nature is, without a doubt, the most *selfish* of qualities. In almost every case it seems to stem either from simple idleness or from a lack of courage. On any other day, at any other moment, my lip would have curled. The scorn I felt would have poured out in torrents. But I was still reeling from what he'd said about me, and couldn't muster the will even to try to confront him. All I could do was pat his hand. I can't remember how the next hour passed. I know I wept. I know that, soon, the two of us were crying in each other's arms. I even have dim memories of hearing myself say soppy things like 'It must be so difficult' and 'I do understand', over and over. I know we were awash in tenderness. I know that, after, we made love.

That evening, Ed rang. 'How is Mr Perfect?'

I'd had my supper. I felt more robust. 'Change of plan,' I informed my brother. 'In future in this respect you may have to ask after the two of us since, from this day on, I aim to out-perfect him.'

'You? Tilly the Wicked Stepmother?'

I was a bit put out. 'What do you mean?'

He tried to backtrack. 'Nothing.'

'Come on, Ed. Spit it out.'

'Nothing, Til. Honestly. It was just a joke.'

'You don't think that I'm horrid to Geoff's children, do you?'

'No, no.' I sensed Ed's discomfort grow as I let silence ride. 'It's just that sometimes . . .'

'Sometimes . . . ?'

'I think you might be just a little scary.'

'Nonsense!'

You can't expect a brother to lose an argument just out of tact. 'It isn't nonsense, Tilly. What about that time when Minna's kitten died?'

'So what about it?'

'Don't you remember? You said she stared up with those waify eyes of hers that get on your nerves so much, and asked if Moppet would be going safely up to Kitten Heaven—'

'Oh, yes.' I felt a tug of shame. 'It's all coming back now.'

But Ed persisted. 'And you said, "Probably. Unless, of course, she's already gone straight down to Kitten Hell."'

'Yes, yes! No need to harp. It was a *joke*.'

'A pretty scary joke, if you're just four.'

'Christ, Ed! Minna must have been at least seven when Moppet got run over!'

'Nevertheless . . .'

Things come to a pretty pass when your own brother thinks you're the monster in the relationship. So, next day, I began afresh. A different person. Someone kind and sensitive. Not like myself. I spent the extra days off work I'd earned in doing things with the children. The hours became a whirl of ice-rinks and films. I cooked their favourite meals as they sat at the table beside me, busily grating and slicing and chopping. I helped them both with their homework, and sat for hours with Minna, cutting things out of magazines and helping her stick them in scrapbooks. To put it bluntly, I was *nice*. I even half enjoyed it. It was a bit like giving up chocolate or meat for Lent: the discipline made me feel all strong and kind and virtuous.

Tilly in Noddyland, you could have called it.

Pity I couldn't keep it up . . .

7

IT'S TRUE WHAT THEY SAY. IF YOU WANT TO BE LOVED, JUST LOVE and be lovable. It is amazing how easily you can win round a child with a bit of attention. Both of them calmed down. Harry still had a terrible problem sleeping, but he stopped being mean to Minna, and seemed more cheerful. Sometimes I was at home. Sometimes I had to go to rigs as far as Texas and Peru. But even from places like that I'd try to keep in touch with cheerful cards posted from airports, and the occasional call. And since I always came home with a gift for each of them – two pretty spinning holograms, hand-carved 'witchdoctor' finger puppets, even boxes of grown-up chocolates – Harry and Minna were soon in the habit of waiting eagerly at the door from the moment they heard the approach of the taxi.

Soon confirmation came that things were going better at school as well. We had a letter from Mrs Dee saying that Harry's behaviour had improved 'immeasurably', and there had been no further incidents involving money gone missing. 'Whatever you're doing,' the letter finished up, 'keep at it, since it's working well.'

We even managed to return the stolen loot. One evening, sitting on the side of the bed, saying goodnight to Harry, I noticed a shadowy streak at the edge of the carpet, as if elves with their very own tiny vacuum cleaner had been raising the nap the wrong way in a line along the skirting. Odd, I thought. Never noticed that before. But even before Harry had finished showing me the fresh graze on his ankle, it had slipped from my mind. Next morning, as I came into the room to dump some laundry, the memory suddenly came back, and I turned round. In daylight, the effect was not so noticeable. Still, it was there, so, dropping to my knees, I ran a fingertip over the narrow strip. Lumps. Actual tiny lumps that I'd have noticed underfoot if they'd been anywhere but there, hard up along the skirting.

I fetched a stubby knife and used the blade to prise up the edge of the carpet. It lifted a whole lot more easily than I expected, and when I peeled it back, there lay a tidy line of coins along the floor beside the skirting. They were grey with dust pounded down through the coarse weave of the carpet backing, but when I picked them up and blew, one or two proved to be new, and one was downright shiny, with that year's date. Most were pound coins, though there was a scattering of other silver. When I added it all up, it came to less than twenty pounds.

It seemed a very small amount of money to make a child of

eleven toss and turn at night, and keep him from that equanimity he needed to get through school. I wondered why Harry hadn't dropped the whole lot down the nearest drain to be rid of the worry, and realized it was his conscience playing up. Stealing the money had been sinful enough. To have thrown it away would have been even more naughty.

I gave both children their juice and cake as usual after school. Then I set Minna up at the table with her ten spellings and her homework reading book, and said to Harry, 'Come with me.'

He followed me up to the little workroom of mine that had become his bedroom. I couldn't see the point in torturing him with a series of questions he had no hope of answering, so I sat on the edge of the bed, pulled him down at my side, and simply pointed. 'See that?'

He went bright scarlet. 'It wasn't *me*,' he wailed. Tears swelled and splashed.

'Yes it was, daftie.'

The tears kept coming. Already the bottom of his shirt was soaked.

'What are we going to do?' I asked. He didn't answer, so I said, 'What I mean is, how are you going to give it back?'

He looked up with a flash of hope. 'Back?'

'Yes. You don't want to have to feel guilty for ever, do you?'

He shook his head.

'Right. So we have to give it back – without,' I added sternly, 'shoving the blame onto someone else.'

He started to cry again.

'All right,' I said. 'I'll do it. I'll go in and give it back and tell that Mrs Dee of yours you're really sorry. But I'll also say that she's got to leave you alone and not talk to you about it. I'll make it clear you only took the money because you're so upset, worrying that your mother might die.'

There. I had done it. I had finally *said* the bloody word. Out loud. To him.

We both sat waiting. In the end, he whispered, 'Will she do that?' And then, before I could make the horrible mistake of answering the wrong question, he carried on hastily, 'Will Mrs Dee really leave me alone and not say anything?'

Interesting, isn't it, the balance of a child's world? That he'd prefer to feel quite safe about his head teacher than use the one and only chance he'd probably yet been offered to ask an honest question about his mother. I was reminded of just how ghastly school can be, and how very much I had hated it.

'I'm sure I can persuade her to let it drop.'

'What about Dad?'

'You leave him to me,' I assured him, knowing full well that no child in his right mind would ever worry for long about trouble emanating from Geoffrey. So that's the plan we followed. I took the money in, and I explained to Mrs Dee. The way I told it, Frances was already halfway into her coffin, and I left Mrs Dee with the impression that, if she said a word to Harry, the poor scrap would almost certainly rush out to hang himself from the first available rafter. In any event, she let the whole business drop. Harry went back to sleeping peacefully. Next time I came home, there was talk of 'merit points' and even, a couple of weeks after that, a spell as 'acting prefect'. I had odd moments of unease. After all, given how fiercely I'd ticked Geoff off for keeping secrets from me, it seemed a little soon to start down the same road myself. But Harry was clearly so much happier pretending the whole sorry mess had never happened, so I, too, put it out of mind on the grounds that I had sorted things out with the minimum upheaval.

And so the weeks went by in growing harmony, and we were all relaxed and happy. Harry and Minna wrote letters to their mother. She rang as often as she could between her yoga classes and having her 'psychic pressure points' massaged, and learning T'ai Chi. 'She's really taking time out to "swim in the waters of Lake Me",' I remember saying once, larding only the slightest veneer of sarcasm onto an expression Frances had used more than once in her letters to the children. 'This must be costing her the bloody *earth*.' Geoff simply shrugged. But I was not surprised when, only a short while later, word came that she was coming home.

'With Terence?'

'No. That's well and truly over. And, anyway, he's only just started his new job.'

Again, it was all news to me. 'Terence? New job?'

Geoff looked a tiny bit rattled. 'Didn't I mention it? It seems he was offered a place at some fancy new medical consultancy in Palo Alto. "Offer he couldn't refuse" sort of thing.'

It didn't sound the level of information commonly gleaned

from children more given to saying things like 'Terence can curl his tongue round like a straw' and 'Terence's mother's cat farts *all the time*'. I couldn't help probing a little. 'How do you know?'

'I can't for the life of me remember.'

'Dad had a letter from him.'

'Really?' I spun round. I hadn't realized Minna was in the doorway.

Neither had Geoff. 'No, I don't think so, poppet.'

Oh, ho! Clearly no female was too young to start being fobbed off by Geoffrey. But, 'Ye-es,' she insisted in a petulant tone I'd not heard from Minna before. 'You gave the stamp to Harry. It had bees on it.'

Good on you, sweetheart, I remember thinking. Starting to grow up at last. But Minna's first tiny stab at stubbornness was lost on Geoffrey. 'Darling, I think you've probably got a bit mixed up.'

'No. You made us toss for it, and Harry won.'

More than one way to skin a cat. 'I have a stamp or two upstairs,' I said. 'I'm pretty sure that one of them has bees on it. Shall we go up and look?'

Did Geoff think I was *stupid*? He didn't even follow us up to the bedroom. So after giving Minna the task of rooting through my messy dressing-table drawer in search of stamps that weren't there, I went through to slide the collector's album I'd bought for Harry out from under his bed, see his fresh acquisition for myself, and realize that, in spite of all my efforts, my place in this family still didn't amount to a heap of beans. Geoff hadn't even bothered to show me the letter Terence had obviously written him – here was the stamp to prove it with its yellow bees – and now his daughter had inadvertently reminded him, he actually preferred to brazen it out than get my opinion about anything in it.

I wasn't going to *beg* to be a real part of this shitty, crumbling family. I handed Minna some old and very pretty Turkish coins to make up for the stamps she couldn't find, then sent her packing. Staying in the bedroom alone, I rang Donald. 'Phone here,' I ordered him. 'Ring in five minutes and say there's been a blow-out and I'm to drop everything to get on the job.' I had a little think. March . . . Beaches . . . 'Tell him the problem's in a rig off Casablanca, and I'm to be back-up on shore.'

Donald burst out laughing. 'Tilly, you're a *monster*. Who's the lucky man?'

The lucky man turned out to be Faisal, the perfect stranger in the bar: rich, well-dressed, smelling of musk and sandalwood. His hands were gentle and his manners perfect. Like Geoff, he went at the business of giving pleasure with at least as much attention as he gave to getting it. Also – and unlike Geoff – he played two-handed bridge and quite liked gambling. After two days, if I hadn't been so off men I do believe that I might even have cancelled my own room, such was my confidence that the rest of the week would continue to be so delicious a pleasure. And I was right.

*

I came home with two thoughts in mind. Never get married. And let bygones be bygones. So you could argue I was in the best of moods when I stepped in the house.

Geoff played his part. 'My God, you look *fantastic*! You look so *tanned*.'

'There was a tremendous amount of hanging about,' I offered, not untruthfully.

'Well, you look *wonderful*.'

We went to bed. I made up quite a lot of stuff about the blow-out (mostly culled from a rather fine disaster video the men had been passing around on the rig a couple of weeks earlier) and the next few days rolled along peacefully enough. Since I was working from home, I took the children skating twice. Then, at the weekend, I went off to visit Mother in the nursing home while Geoff took Minna and Harry round to see Frances, who had just flown home.

I was gone no more than a couple of hours. Still, when I got back, supper was already in the offing. I sniffed the air and called out, 'Whatever it is, it smells *delicious*.'

Geoff popped his head round the kitchen door. 'I hope you're hungry. I've made heaps. Far too much.'

I had a kind thought. 'You could take some round to Frances.'

Clenching his wooden spoon in his mouth as if he were a Spaniard biting a long-stemmed rose, Geoff did a couple of flamenco heel clicks and took my coat. 'Just what I planned.'

'Why? Is she looking peaky? Has she lost more weight?'

'She looked quite well, I thought.'

I found that hard to credit. 'Really? Quite well? Or "quite well, considering"?'

'Quite well, considering,' he had to admit. Then he went all the way. 'Actually, she looks bloody awful.'

'Will she be able to cope?'

'She says she thinks so.'

'I'm glad,' I said. (I did sincerely wish her well.) And that was when Geoff put his foot straight in it. 'Yes. Listen, Til. I know I should have asked you first, but I did say to Frances that, if she can't manage, then we'll have Harry and Minna back.'

'Back?' I glanced round. Sure enough, in the short time that I'd been out of the house, all Minna's cut-outs had vanished from the hall table. The sports gear wasn't in the corner. The coat rack looked less colourful and cluttered. 'What? Have they gone already? Without even saying goodbye?'

'Oh. Sorry. I didn't think.'

For a moment I went blank. Then – think of a live wire on the loose. The question is, will it touch anything? If it does, hair will startle and skin will fry. And, if it doesn't, no one would know the difference. I'm not quite sure how long I stood there, wondering where to go next in this quite hopeless quest to make this man see me, not just as some living, breathing instrument of use to him and his family, but as a human being in my own right, with actual feelings. It took a while to gather courage to look his way. But, when I did, I saw him eyeing me uneasily in the hall mirror. He'd worked out that he'd blown it yet again. All he was wondering now was which form the attack would take, and when it would come.

And I couldn't be bothered. It was as simple as that. I couldn't raise the energy to make the effort. As all the fellows on the rig would say, 'Shit, or get off the pot.' The man was *hopeless*. Either he was thick or he was stubborn. I found it hard to believe that someone with brains enough to tie his shoelaces could be so stupid as to continually fail to learn from experience. But there you are. It had to be a possibility. The only alternative was that he was determined to make it crystal clear that he was always to be in total control of any decision relating to his former wife and children, whatever the cost to the two of us.

But, given the way he blinded himself, whenever convenient, to those children's emotions, that seemed unlikely.

No, he must be thick.

So there I stood, watching him in the mirror watching me. The moments passed. I thought about how men talk on the rig. How, when you listen, it becomes quite clear they have a gift for shoving separate chunks of their lives into separate boxes. (Look at Sol. Loved me, and quite sincerely loved his wife.) Men who would kick themselves for idiots if they designed a drill system with no regard for the pumps, or planned a draining line without a thought for the electrics, can blunder their way through their personal lives like utter imbeciles, seemingly incapable of taking more than one person's feelings into account at any one time.

So. The same old hairy question. Stay, or go? Tick, tick. I watched poor Geoff endure each waiting moment like a man who can't breathe till the guillotine falls.

Meanwhile, the smell of casserole filled up the hall.

'What are you cooking?'

He fell on the straw he'd been offered. '*Boeuf bourgignon*. I thought we should celebrate having the house back to ourselves.' He couldn't wait to take the chance to steer away from danger. 'I made a berry *pannacotta* too, and there's some of that heavenly cheese we keep finding at Lacey's.'

I straightened up and told myself: Right, Til. You work on and off oil rigs, so it could fairly be argued that, at least in part, you are a rigger. And at a moment like this, what would a rigger say and do?

Nothing more to decide. 'Jolly good!' I said. 'Foul visit to the nursing home. Horrible disapproving nurse and Mum more bats than ever. It seemed to drag on for hours. I'm bloody starving. How long will supper be?'

I clearly hadn't put aside all power of feeling. When I saw Frances the following weekend, my heart went out to her, clinging to the side of her front door, looking so thin, drawn and shaky.

The children rushed past her into the house, late for some telly show. I hung about, pretending to have a problem with the strap of my shoe, till they were out of earshot. Then, 'Sure that you'll be all right?' I asked. 'It can't be a picnic without Terence here to help. Can't I send Geoff round to mow your lawn, or bring you some groceries, or something?'

'No, really, Tilly. Thanks. I am managing.' She switched hands on the door, ready to shuffle back in the house. Then she said, over her shoulder, 'Oh, there is one thing. If you could just make sure he doesn't forget to pick me up on Wednesday.'

I didn't blink. 'Wednesday.'

'Three fifteen should be fine.'

'Three fifteen. Right.'

I went back to my car, waved and drove off. Three days till Wednesday, all without the children. Twice we had leisurely meals in which the words 'Oh, by the way, Til, did I remember to tell you what's happening on Wednesday?' would have fitted in as well as any other.

But nothing. Nothing. Not a peep.

The fact is, you can make all the grand decisions you want to put aside one failing part of your relationship – be lofty, even – decide what you value most, and let the rest go hang. The problem is, only the dead can do it. Nobody else can keep it up. The world is crawling with people who told themselves, 'I know my partner's a jerk. But this is a nice house, and children need two parents. I'll hold tight.' What happens? Within a day or two the pudding plates are flying because he's said the wrong thing yet again, or she has made the exact same mistake he'd known from the start she would make. The fact is, feelings *matter*. So I make no apologies for watching Geoffrey like a hawk, smiling invitingly over our intimate suppers (Oh, go on, Geoffrey. You can talk to me. It's perfectly safe.) and even switching round my next few days on rig so I would definitely be there on Wednesday.

From the impassive way Geoff started the day, you'd have thought nothing would happen. In the morning he shot into town, but that was just for batteries for his camera, and he was back within the hour. I made the lunch. I let the conversation dangle, making a point of showing I was in an easy mood, and leaving giant gaps in which the words 'Oh, by the way, Tilly . . .' would fall as naturally as morning rain.

They only came as he was going out of the door at two o'clock. 'Oh, by the way, Til. I want to swing round the suppliers this afternoon to pick up a few things. If you're around, can you let in the children?'

Bugger the children. By three I was sitting in my car round the corner from Frances's house. Geoff's car had to pass me on the one-way street. I watched it sail by and pulled out to follow, knowing I didn't really need to keep the two of them strictly in view on the short journey. After all, where else would the pair be headed in term-time, halfway through the afternoon, except to their children's school?

I only bothered to hang around so I could see how long the meeting lasted. (Over an hour.) Geoff had to drop off Frances, so I was home first. 'You got in the house all right, then?' I congratulated Minna, nodding at the door key she'd left on the side.

She was triumphant. 'Harry had forgotten. He looked under all the wrong flowerpots. I kept on telling him, "It's that one, Harry," but he wouldn't listen. And I was right.' She didn't notice I was barely listening. 'Look, Tilly. I'm making another glitter picture. It's a princess.'

Across the top of her thick sheet of paper, she ran a smear of glue, then picked up her tiny tube of glitter and sprinkled on silver. Raising the edges, she tipped and blew until she had a shower of twinkling stardust across her painted navy sky. 'Do you know what that is?'

'Radioactive dust?' I asked sourly, startling her mightily.

Out in the garden, Harry was lying backwards across the plank bottom of the plaited rope swing, letting it untwist. 'The clouds are spinning, Tilly.'

He didn't see my face because he was leaning back so far his hair brushed the ground. 'Til, when you went off to big school, did they ever flush your head down the lavatory?'

New one on me. But, on the track of information myself, I thought it prudent to offer a soothing answer. 'No. There was a good deal of talk about it in my primary school, but once we all moved up to secondary, nothing ever happened.'

Relieved, he hauled himself upright and smiled. I took a chance, and went fishing. 'So, Harry, what do you think they'll all decide today?'

'Who?'

Was he just checking? 'You know. Your mum and dad and Mrs Dee.'

'Oh, *them*.' He sighed. 'It isn't just Mrs Dee,' he told me gravely. 'It's *all* the teachers. And I think they'll agree that I'll be better off at Park Place School than Wallace Secondary.'

'Less head-flushing?'

He pouted. 'And more exams. And horrid purple blazers. And sports all Saturday morning.' He sighed. And it was only as an afterthought he tacked it on. 'But Gran says that she thought the tennis courts were *brilliant*.'

I took it gently. After all, she might have simply seen a catalogue. 'So Granny went round the school with your mother?'

'And Dad.'

See? 'And Dad.' Say what you like about deciding not to care, these things will send their poisonous bubbles up through any coating of tranquillity, however well laid down. A fucking *nerve*, to fix a time when Granny – who was barely on the radar – could look around a school, but not take me, who had looked after them for five whole months, and given up the one room in the house I used to still call mine, and made such efforts to be good to them.

Good job that Harry was back to spinning, and didn't see the look on my face. 'Til? What's insurance?'

God, what a question. 'It's just money you pay in, and the insurance company gives you a whole lot more back if something bad happens.'

'What sort of something bad? Like someone dying?'

Even through my distraction, alarm bells rang. I did my best. 'Yes, I suppose so.' To make it clear he might be worryng in vain, I added, 'Or the house burning down. Or the car crashing. Or stepping on your watch. Or losing your wallet.'

But he was on the ball, as usual. 'Gran said to Mum, if they decide to send me to Park Place, she ought to think about taking out insurance for the school fees. And Mum snapped back at her and said, "I'm not dead yet, thanks! I think I'll just take my chances."'

'Good on your mother,' I said absently, still brooding on the fact that, yet again, I'd been left out of things.

Harry pulled himself upright to give me one of his searching looks. Then, falling back again, he launched into quite a long speech. 'I *thought* you'd say that. You often stick up for Mum, don't you, Tilly? Connor's dad's girlfriend is horrible about *his* mum. His dad says he's to ignore it, and just not listen. But you quite like Mum, don't you? She says you even told her you'd send Dad round to do the garden for her if she can't manage. So you must like her a bit.'

'Oh, yes. I have no problems with your mother.'

So what *should* I have said? The actual *truth*? That I had covered for the stupid cow through all her half-brained shiatsu and her reiki, her idiot zen, her numerology crap, her daft magnetic therapy and, for all I knew, classes in bloody runes. And in return, she and her unthinking ex-mate had fixed up to choose a school without the very person who would have to care for her son if (more than likely, *when*) her little cancer cells came back in force.

I really didn't have a lot of choice. Harry was only twelve. How can you tell a boy that age that you wish *both* his bloody parents dead?

Sadly – you can't.

8

BUT YOU CAN BROOD. BROOD ON THE REASONS YOU MIGHT still be around. It clearly wasn't anything to do with why women usually stay, grimly prepared to get less from a partnership simply because they need that partnership more. After all, it was my house. I had my freedom and a salary, and I can fix the washer. Someone like me had to think again. And think I did. I gave up idly blaming all those other things – the timelessness of sky and sea, Geoff's kindness and caresses, even the tempting smell of casserole – for the fact that I stayed with a man I was coming to despise (and at times truly hated). Gradually I came round to facing the truth.

Living with Geoff suited me.

The thing is, I am not a nice person. (That, or I'm normal and no one else tells the truth.) Way back in primary school, I used to pray for the death of Ingrid Molloy. She was everything I longed to be: blond, sweet and clever. (It turned out I was

clever too, but no one had realized.) So every night I lit the
candle stub that I kept hidden, and prayed for Ingrid's death. I
didn't pray to God. Even to me, that would have seemed a
dreadful blasphemy. And I did not admit to myself I prayed to
the Devil. But I'm not sure who else I might have thought
would use his powers to make her drown, or eat a poisoned tart,
or fall under the wheels of the school bus. Each morning I
greeted Ingrid with a cheery smile, sat at the desk beside her,
shared my sweets, joined in the games she played, and quite
enjoyed her company.

The only thing was that I wanted her *gone*.

So maybe I have an inbuilt leaning to ambivalence. But
Geoff did play his part. Oh, he was unfailingly charming and
kind, still treating me each day as if I were a precious gift that
had, by sheer good fortune, come to him. But underneath, with
all his petty betrayals, all his small deceptions, you might have
thought he was in two minds too, and deliberately seeding the
weeds that would rise up and choke us.

Because, as months passed, it became more and more clear
to me that there are real advantages in sharing life with someone so determinedly denying you the one thing you want. It
makes you feel quite justified in being selfish back, and for
someone like me, that is very much an asset. Doing exactly
what I want has always come naturally. Indeed, I take it rather
as a virtue, remembering with a shudder my Aunty Jean, who
was forever twisting herself out of shape trying to do the very
best by everyone and, under the strain of it, turning into a
harpy. I think, too, of Ed's former wife, who was continually

asking visitors what they would like to do, or eat. 'No, honestly. That's fine by me. I would have chosen that too.' Even in other people's houses she was quite intolerable, responding to every single question with another. 'So are you hungry yet, Alice?' 'How about you?' 'Would you care for a walk?' 'Is that what *you* feel like doing?' Spending a weekend with Alice was like an endless round of Liars' Dice, with all the polite fibs and the second-guessing – and with, as often as not, the creeping and dispiriting suspicion that no one in the room was either getting what they really wanted, or even the pale satisfaction of being sure that someone else was taking pleasure in their stead.

So there was something to be grateful for in facing facts. The woman Geoffrey loved was not the one who stood before him, flawed but real; it was some pedestal job, some figment of his boyish fantasies, unsuitable for grown-up life. Starved of the openness on which a relationship thrives, ours quietly shrivelled, till I was having more honest conversations with Donald in the company office than ever I had with Geoffrey. 'Poor bloody bugger.' Donald kept sticking up for him. 'You should be glad you've got him.' (Echoes of Ed.) And I would shrug, finding it hard to explain that in a way I was. And not just glad. Grateful. Because, as time passed, there was something more and more beguiling about being left to hide in silence and work. All the convenience of a second body in the house ('Could you help with this ladder?' 'While you're in town, would you pick up some milk?') but none of the frustration and effort of engagement.

Our conversations, which, when real, so often used to sour, now turned more easy and affectionate. I found it restful, and it made decisions easy. I did exactly as I chose, feeling no guilt, for after all a partner cannot cherry-pick their way through life. And since all Geoff's decisions over the last few years had made it clear he gave me no real standing in Harry and Minna's lives, I took it as fair dealing he couldn't interfere in mine.

'Off to North Africa? For three *months*? Tilly, can't you say no?'

I made a face. 'That might be difficult. I mean, there's such a power struggle going on between the contractors and the service company. I'm sure as soon as it's sorted they'll stop squeezing my schedule. But in the meantime . . .'

'There must be *someone* who could go instead.'

I shrugged. 'I'm sorry. Right now, there just aren't enough of us to pick and choose.' He still looked doubtful, so I added airily, 'You know – what with the cream-off of good engineers to all this new wind-farm technology.'

Bollocks on stilts, but he bought it. 'You will be back in time for Christmas?'

'Of course I will. Probably before, if all this spatting between the contractors stops.' I gave him a smile. I felt quite sorry for him, knowing he would be lonely. He hardly saw the kids now. Each week they acted more and more offhand, constantly cancelling mid-week visits – even whole weekends – because of things they wanted to do more: hanging around shopping malls, having sleepovers with friends, going on school trips to France. Whatever strides Harry made towards independence, Minna seemed almost instantly in his wake. It was as if the gap in age between the two of them was fading to nothing. And as time passed it somehow gradually became more and more difficult to stay plugged in to any of the small progressions of their lives: Harry's first set of real exams; Minna's attempts to get in the county swimming team. In the absence of regular updates, even the seemingly endless decisions about which subjects each child should study further and which should be dropped became hard to discuss. Soon, both had become so leggy, so forthright, so very independent, that it was difficult even to get them to phone when they weren't going to make the effort to show up and sleep over.

'You ought to be pleased,' I tried to comfort Geoff. 'It's good they're ready to stand on their own feet. This is the age when young people are supposed to break away and need their parents less.'

He looked so wistful. 'Tilly, do you suppose, if you and I had had children . . .'

I can't bear maudlin sentimentality. In the old days, I would have pulled him up with acid talk of living in Noddyland. Now, I used simple distraction. 'How about trying bribery? Teenagers love showing off. Why don't you invite them somewhere really special and tell them each can bring a friend?'

'What sort of somewhere special?'

'Tatiana's? Or The Oyster Bed?'

He looked embarrassed. 'As it happens, Til, I'm a bit short this month.'

'I'll pay.'

So that's what we did. At least the two of them showed up. It worked a treat. Harry and Minna were all over their father, and more forthcoming than they'd been for as long as I could remember. Even the presence of the inarticulate and staring friends wasn't a problem. So over the next couple of years we fell into the habit of dealing with the business of getting to see them by offering lunches or dinners out. After a while, I couldn't help but notice that arrangements for any old pizza joint or cheap Mexican dive were as often as not cancelled. ('Sorry, Dad. Something's come up.') It had to be fancy French restaurants. Smart Italian places. And it was in one of these, Giovanni's, that one day I caught sight of Sol, a little older and a whole lot stockier after the missing years, lunching with two other men in the corner.

Our eyes met. Neither of us smiled or waved, making it clear, as Sol said afterwards, that both of us were in the market for a touch of discretion. I admit I had no real need to get up from my seat and go off to the Ladies. And it was no surprise to find him lurking in the vestibule when I came out.

'Sol!'

'Tilly! As lovely as ever.' Taking my outstretched hand in both of his, he turned it over, bent to kiss the palm, then pressed into it one of his lavish business cards with raised gold lettering. 'See you soon, sweetheart.' He vanished into the men's room.

I looked at the card. New office address, new phone number, and, when I turned it over, scribbled on the back: 'Phone me.'

Was it so clear-cut that I would? To Sol, perhaps. As for myself, I went round and round the houses offering myself excuses. The conversation that I'd tried to have with Geoff about what should happen to his father's house, now the old bugger had died. ('I think I'll take my time on this one, Tilly.') The forceful attempt I'd made to get him to talk to the children when Frances's cancer came back in force. ('I think, what with their exams coming up, I'd rather leave it a while.') Every attempt to live in the real world seemed strangled at birth. Why, only that morning Geoff had muttered, 'Not the best day for a long lunch, as it happens. I'm a bit pushed,' and I had answered cheerfully enough, 'Well, if you want Harry and Minna to cry off, just send a message that we've switched the venue to Mexican Joe's.'

He'd rounded on me in an instant. 'That's a bit mean, Til.'

'It's the truth.'

'Not as I see it,' he'd responded in a huff, and left the room on the excuse of fetching some pair of socks out of the drier. I'd sat on the bed, I remember, pulling on my tights and tipping my head from side to side like a small clockwork doll as I ran through his repertoire of tired phrases, all designed to make the point that he didn't agree with me without going to the trouble of trying to persuade me.

'That's a bit harsh.' 'Not my experience.' 'I'm surprised that you think that.' I swung my head faster and faster, like a metronome gone mad, and threw in the lofty disbelieving eyebrow that so annoyed me. 'Honestly, Tilly, you do say the oddest things!' 'I know you can't really believe that.' 'Oh, Tilly. I take it that's a joke.' By the time Geoff came thundering back up the stairs with his socks, the doll face I'd been making must have degenerated into that of a staring maniac.

He caught me muttering, 'I think it's best I ignore that,' in a mechanical voice.

'Are you all right?' he asked.

'Fine,' I assured him. 'Never better. Just seeing if I can say "if you say so, dear" in twenty different languages.'

To me, that is the sort of challenge a partner should stand up to meet. ('What are you saying, Tilly? That I just fob you off?') But Geoff chose to pretend he hadn't heard. 'You'd better get your skates on or we'll be late.'

So I could argue I have Geoff to thank for pretty well driving me back into Sol's arms. And Sol to thank in turn for keeping Geoff and me together over the next few years. Sometimes it was a matter of an afternoon, sometimes a whole weekend tacked onto the end of a few days on rig or slid in before the inspections. The company put their foot in it once or twice, phoning to ask if I could take over for people who had failed to show up, or gone off sick. More than once, Geoffrey met me at the door to take my coat and ask in a puzzled fashion, 'Everything all right? Someone rang trying to get you. They seemed to think you flew home yesterday.'

I'd play it supercool. 'Really? I shall be pretty pissed off if they fuss about last night's hotel bill.'

Off Geoff would trot, persuaded both by my indifference and by his own need never to look trouble in the eye. And that's how Sol became a pressure valve. Each time I needed someone to agree with me that facts were facts, Sol played the game.

Out of a sense of fairness I offered each conversation to Geoff first. 'Guess what I've just seen. Minna, in the queue for the Odeon ticket office. Shouldn't she be in school?'

'That happens to me all the time, Til. I keep thinking I see one or other of them all over town. It is amazing how alike young people look.'

'Geoff, while you were out, somebody's mother rang. She wasn't very coherent. She wouldn't leave her name and she was in a real temper. But she said Harry's been offering her daughter "substances", and if it happens again, she's going to report it.'

'Harry? Ridiculous!'

'Aren't you even going to ask him?'

'I wouldn't insult him in that way.'

'Geoff—'

'No, Til!' His colour rose. 'One can be all too quick to think the worst of young people.'

So it was to Sol that I turned for sensible discussion of irritations through Harry and Minna's teenage years: Minna's persistent truancy; Harry's strange, quiet slidings on and off the rails. Often Sol ticked me off for not tackling their problems a whole lot more forcibly. 'Teenagers these days live in a dangerous world, Tilly. Parents have to stay on top of them. You must *make* Geoff listen.'

'You underestimate the man. If he prefers to live in Happy Valley, nothing will shift him.'

'But it's so bad for Harry and Minna. Don't you *care?*'

'Sol, if I wanted something to worry myself sick about night and day, I'd have had kids of my own '

Sol came out with the echoes of Donald and Ed I'd heard so often since we'd picked up again. 'You're a cold fish, Til. And if you can't be bothered to kick the man into being someone you can respect, you ought to do the decent thing and let the poor bugger go.'

'There speaks the man who's ratting on his own wife!'

Sol shook a finger. 'That's the whole point, Tilly. I *adore* Lydia. We have an entire life built up. Our son, my daughters and a lovely house—'

'I know! I know! Your splendid antique furniture. All her nice jewellery. Your place in France.'

He leaned back against the pillows. 'Exactly! A life shared – that's what we have.' He ran a finger down my naked breast. 'All except you, of course. And what have you got in common with Geoffrey? Nothing. You're even too mean-spirited to marry him. Give him a break, Tilly. Set the poor sod free to find a nicer woman while he still has time. Do the right thing. Dump the poor bastard.'

I rolled away. 'And just become one of your playthings? No thanks, Sol.'

But later, driving home, I gave the idea some real thought. What Sol said did make sense. How would Geoff feel if, after Harry and Minna finally grew up and became absorbed in their own lives, I was to stir myself enough to leave? Unless I thought we'd be together till the bitter end, then it was better, surely, to put an end to things now, not do it later and feel terrible because I'd left him all alone.

But in the end, as usual, I let the whole thing ride for the most trivial reason. Donald rang to say he'd found the perfect car for Harry: battered to bits on the outside, but sound as a bell. It seemed a shame to give the lad something so perfect for his birthday, then disappear at once. So, when I could over the next few weeks, I'd pick him up from Frances's and drive him to the abandoned aerodrome beside a storage plant of ours a few miles north. Once or twice he turned up in a suspiciously elated mood. (Once, after the briefest look at him, I faked excuses and I drove straight home.) But, on the whole, the boy was all attention and all charm throughout the lessons, and got so good at handling the car that I used to leave him to it and sit, reading, on a wall till he was ready to go home. He took his test a fortnight after his next birthday, and phoned up, crowing. 'Easy-peasy, Til! And the examiner even shook my hand after she passed me!'

From that day on, like Geoffrey, I was back out in the cold. In fact things were worse, for now when Minna needed driving anywhere, instead of phoning Geoff, as she always had before, Frances simply asked Harry to take his sister. After the car I bought him ended up smashed beyond repair in some ditch, she took to nodding at him to take the keys to her own. And since, in the grip of her treatments, Frances no longer had the will or energy to pay attention to just how often her son was emptying her purse to fill up the tank, Harry took full advantage, persuading his sister to say she needed to go into Newcastle time and again when he felt like a jaunt with his friends. Geoffrey would mope. 'I never see them these days.' It didn't bother me. I just got on with my own life. Each time my brother rang, he made a point of asking, 'And how are Harry and Minna?' Again and again I'd spoon out the same deflecting answer. So it came almost as a surprise to hear myself saying one evening, 'Oh, they're both fine. But as it happens, Frances is back in hospital so tonight we're taking them out.'

'Somewhere nice?'

'Pretty swish, yes.'

'Your money's still growing on trees, then?'

'Not half.'

And maybe it was because the image of a money tree stuck in my mind that, when I watched Geoffrey fruitlessly scrabbling through his pockets for his credit card at the end of the evening, it struck me that almost every time, these days, it was me who ended up reaching across to slide the bill towards my coffee cup, and get the business of paying over and done with so we could leave.

It set me thinking yet again about the printing shop. Right from the start I had been mystified by Print-It! I'd had this view, presumably gleaned from Sol, that little businesses were always either 'going up' or 'going down'; yet in the years that Geoff and I had been together, he'd never said a word that might lead anyone to think the small shop on the High Street was anything other than a steady thing that simply kept rolling along with his hand on the tiller. He never seemed to go in more or go in less. He never agonized over whether to manage without Mrs Mackie, or ask Doris to work extra hours. He never stayed there late to finish things, and I could only ever recall him rushing back to the shop on his free afternoon if one of the copiers had broken. Thinking about it more carefully I realized, too, that I had never known Geoff seek out business advice, or buy any of those books you see all over airports, or even pore over work spreadsheets. It came to mind that when we'd first got together I'd left the business sections of the newspaper lying about, presuming that, like Sol, he did at least run his eyes over the various articles and predictions. But after a while, seeing the inserts lying still folded, unopened, day after day, I'd started dropping them straight in the bin just as I had before, and not a word was ever said. I don't believe Geoff even noticed.

And there were other things that made him seem far more like someone else's happy-go-lucky employee than a man who held the fate of a business in his hand. When I asked idly, 'How's it going at the shop?' he'd always answer, 'Pretty busy this week,' or, 'Quite slack today,' as if the amount of photocopying passing through was the important thing, not any overarching pattern of profit or loss. It made me curious, and for the very first time I realized that, if we had merged our finances, it would have made me most uneasy. But we had stayed apart on money matters, and he kept all his paperwork packed away. Indeed, the only negotiation between us I could even recall was when, right at the start, it was agreed that Geoff should shove more money in the communal pot to make up for the fact that I was making payments for the roof over our heads while he was still pocketing rent from his own flat.

So I had no excuse to pry. But now, as time passed, I became suspicious. Twice, Geoff borrowed quite large amounts of money from me and had to be reminded to pay it back. He took to blaming our local cash machine more and more often for the fact he was short of cash over a weekend, and I heard him chasing customers about the sort of bills he used to leave to gather dust. Almost in spite of myself, I started taking an interest in what came through the letterbox. I was there less than half of the time, of course. But, now my attention had been drawn to it, I noticed that almost nothing came for Geoff. Most bills were still in my own name regardless of which of us paid them. But other things I would have expected to see – his bank and credit card statements, offers from loan companies, pension stuff, anything to do with the flat – none of it arrived any more. I even looked for paperwork for his father's house. (I'd remembered it falling in heaps on our mat after the old man's funeral.) But there was nothing. I even found myself wondering if

Geoff had opened a box number somewhere without telling me. Or taken to using his work address to receive all his own mail.

One night, I asked him casually, 'Can you remember who owned Print-It! before you?'

'It was a Mrs Bellacosa. Why?'

'Oh,' I said, shrugging, 'I just remembered that she had a pretty name and couldn't recall what it was.' I prodded a shred of lettuce with my fork. 'Why did she pack it in?'

'Retired, I think.'

'What, back to sunnier climes, clutching her fortune?'

'No fortunes in bloody printing!'

He had such a grim look on his face that I felt pity. I didn't press the matter. If I am honest, I didn't want to give him the chance to ask me for money. I had a horrid feeling that any cash he took from me now would never be paid back.

That night, I phoned Ed. 'Can I talk to you about Mum's money? I rather think Geoff might be on the verge of asking me to lend him quite a bit of it.'

Ed might have been fond of Geoff, but he wasn't stupid. 'Is it the business? Is it going under?'

I didn't answer. I just cut to the chase. 'Whatever he asks, Ed, you do promise that you'll say no? Absolutely not. *Nada*.'

'We have joint power of attorney, Tilly. You can tell him yourself.'

'Ed, I have to *live* with him. It will be so much easier if you're the Big Bad Wolf.'

He didn't take persuading. He knew as well as I did that,

batty as she was, Mum might hang on for years and, once her money had run out, it would be some grim hospital, his house or mine. 'No worries, Tilly. I'll be as hard as nails. The man won't get a bean out of me.'

Or out of anyone else with any business sense, it seemed. Over the next four weeks, Geoff changed suppliers twice. (He had a lot of airy-fairy reasons, but when I checked with Sol, he said it almost certainly would have been because they'd stopped offering credit. 'Don't lend him any loot, Til. It'll be money down the drain.')

Then Doris, who had worked for Geoff for almost eleven years, was suddenly 'looking round for another job'. That's why I didn't hear alarm bells ring at once when she rang up one morning. 'Is Geoff there?'

'He left ten minutes ago. He should be with you any min—'

But she'd already interrupted to tell me her salary hadn't gone into her account on the day that it should have. Even before I could decide which tack to take, she added hurriedly, 'Ah, here he comes. No need to mention it, Tilly. I can ask him about it myself.'

I looked at my watch and it was only five to nine. I'm not the sort of woman to monitor her partner's day, but after all those years I knew enough to be quite sure he rarely reached the shop before ten past the hour. So why had Doris rung at all? Was it to let me know? To give me warning?

It was the next call that brought me hard up against the facts. I'd scarcely put down the phone before it rang again. This time, it was Frances. Instead of following up her usual indifferent 'Oh. Hi, Tilly' with the traditionally dismissive 'I think I'll phone back later', she asked me meaningfully, 'Nice meal out?'

'It was quite good,' I admitted. 'We hadn't been to Shrimps before, and I was impressed.'

'Nice prices, too, as I've heard.'

'No, it wasn't cheap.'

The crunch came. 'Frankly, I'm rather surprised that Geoff can pay his way at all these fancy restaurants – given he's just announced he won't be able to pay his whack when Harry goes through college.'

I could have cheered her up. 'Geoff? Pay his way?' I could have said, 'You must be joking.' But right from the start she'd been as good as Geoff at cutting me out of things. Live by the sword, die by the sword, I say. 'Well, Frances,' I responded cheerfully, 'you know the two of you have always preferred to leave me out of everything to do with their education. So I wouldn't know.'

That night, remembering all the times Ed had accused me of going at poor Geoff too hard, I came at it sideways. 'Don't you ever wish you could just close up shop and walk away?'

'What's up, Til? Fed up with pumping systems and submersible drilling units?'

And into the braking lane went that conversation. So I was quite surprised when, less than an hour after brazening that one out, Geoff sidled up and asked, 'You couldn't lend me a bit of money, could you?'

'What, for the weekend?'

He looked embarrassed. 'A bit more than that. To tide the business over a bad patch.'

'What sort of bad patch?'

'Oh, you know. You only need a couple of people who won't settle bills for things to get sticky.'

'Bad debts? I'll sort them out for you.' (I'd learned that knack from Sol. He used to make me phone up customers in a bored sort of sing-song to 'chcck an address', and when the person asked why I wanted it, give the name of a notorious collection service or, to real innocents, say I was phoning from the County Court. It used to work a treat.)

'I'll bring the details home.'

He never did. So we just waited. Once or twice I sympathetically brought up the subject of the 'bad patch'. But he affected not to hear, and soon it became clear that the only way Geoffrey wanted to take money from me was with me offering it with a sweet and trusting wifely smile, along with an old-fashioned 'Here you are, dear. A chunk of my old mother's savings. I'm sure that you know best. Do with it what you will.'

Fat bloody chance of that.

The next few weeks, I felt like The Ice Queen. It wasn't pleasant. I did what I could – bought treats, kept coming out with, 'Let's go out for supper. My shout tonight.' I kept both cars topped up with petrol and even cancelled my crack-of-dawn taxi once or twice so I could drop in at some supermarket on the long drive home and pack the car sky high with groceries, and all the other supplies it takes to keep a house running. I must have kept Geoff's day-to-day expenses down to almost nothing. But still the crunch came. One night, Geoffrey spread his hands across the table and said: 'I don't know what I'm going to do.'

To me, all problems are the same. They're technical – to do with how systems flow: gas, oil, power, money. Geoff looked relieved to bring his bits of paperwork to the table, and I was careful not to remark on the discreet little box number at the top of so many. I started drawing up my tidy charts. Owed. Owing. Overheads. None of the amounts seemed critical. 'Are you quite sure that this is everything?' I must have asked him half a dozen times. 'There's nothing else? No money lenders sitting up darkened alleys, waiting for cash? No loans on ice?'

He shook his head. 'No, that's the lot.'

The man looked so forlorn, I searched for comfort for him. 'Never mind. These debts aren't all that crippling. You can get rid of most of them at a stroke.'

'How?'

'Selling the flat, of course.'

I *know* I said that. I've the clearest memory because, the instant the words were out of my mouth, I felt so trapped. What if I wanted him to leave? What if I quarrelled horribly with one of his children? What if I fell in love?

Clearly I'd missed his next words. 'What was that?' I asked.

'I said I'd rather take a loan from you.'

Tartly, I rubbed his nose in it. 'You mean, from my mother's savings for her old age?'

'I suppose so.'

Not wanting Ed's refusal to come as too much of a shock, I tried to introduce a businesslike tone of my own. 'What, against the security of 2A Tanner Street?'

He seemed a little miffed. 'Of course.'

I gathered up the papers. 'Let's take a break.'

I found some wine. We had a pleasant evening. I even took him to bed to cheer him up, and, when he was fast asleep after, crept down to run through my fax copier the bulk of the papers he'd shown me, and one or two others I found in his briefcase.

Next day, I made a date with Sol.

'What, *now?*' he grumbled. (I could practically see him scowling at his watch.)

'If you don't mind. I am supposed to be in Aberdeen by crack of dawn tomorrow.'

When I arrived, he was still grumbling. 'Christ, Tilly! We're supposed to see each other for a bit of nookie, not for more bloody *work*.'

'Just do your stuff, Sol. Your reward will come in heaven.'

He spread the papers. Tapping his pencil against his teeth, he stared at the figures. After a while, he reached for the bank statements I'd filched from the briefcase and leafed his way forward and back through the pile.

'Tilly, see these?' He lifted the sheets, one by one, his pencil coming down, month by month, against one payment.

'Doesn't seem much,' I offered.

'No. But it's to a mortgage-lending company.'

I leaned across to point to another entry. 'I think you'll find this is his mortgage payment.'

'I think you'll find he has another now. A supplementary.'

'Against his flat?'

'My guess. And, if Print-It! goes under, this lot take Tanner Street, and that is that.'

I was quite shocked. But pride came to the fore. All of those times when Solly sat in bed and lectured me about the flaws in my relationship came back in force. I didn't want him to see how much humiliation I was feeling, so played it down, trying to act as if, when you're unmarried and don't have children together, you hardly find it surprising when big financial decisions take place while you're working abroad, or busy with other things.

Still, simple astonishment can't be quelled entirely. 'Thank Christ for Briar Cottage!'

There was a gleam in Solly's eye. 'Briar Cottage?'

'His father's place. Geoff has been havering about what to do with it since the day of the funeral.' I tried to look on the bright side. 'At least, now he'll have to sell it, I can stop nagging him about leaving it empty.'

I saw Sol looking at me pityingly.

'What?' I said.

'See here?'

Leaning against his shoulder, I watched Sol's stubby fingers walk back through statement after statement. Even I couldn't help but notice the figure in the last column was fattening steadily as he ploughed back through the months. Sol's finger stopped beside a figure bloated out so far it grazed the column edge.

We sat in silence for a little while, then I said: 'Briar Cottage?'

'I can't think what else.'

I checked the date. '*That* long ago? Almost as soon as he inherited it.'

Now Sol was walking his fingers back the other way, dropping each printed sheet in turn as the column we had been watching grow now took to shrivelling. 'Dribbled away,' he said forlornly, rather as if the money had come from his very own coffers. 'That is the problem with men like him. They form an image of themselves as "businessmen", and won't let go of it. Even when the facts are staring them in the face, they'll let every last asset run through their fingers rather than sell the place to someone smarter who could make a go of it.'

I felt my first small twinge of hope. 'Someone like you?'

Sol sighed. 'Not promising. I'd have to nose around a bit first. But it's a prime site.' He peered at me quizzically over his reading glasses. 'I take it he wouldn't be wanting any more for it than being kept out of Queer Street.'

'He can go over a fucking cliff for all I care!'

'Now, now, Til,' Sol reproved me. 'Nobody benefits from having to step over old partners in the gutter. Best get him on his feet again before you decide if you want to plant the boot on his backside.'

Decide? Already my only concern was that Sol should

help me cobble together enough of a raft from the wreckage to cast Geoff adrift. But all I said was, 'Ever the cool adviser, eh, Sol?'

'Hard head, that's all. "You pays your money and you takes your choice."'

He held a hand out and we went to bed. I wasn't really in the mood, but Geoff deserved it. What a fucking liar! How many times had I asked, 'Is this *all*?' How many times had he assured me, 'Yes, that's everything,' and sat there hoping I'd whip out the chequebook to my mother's account, assuming his old flat and Briar Cottage would be security against all risk. Don't people who evade hard truth have any limits at all? Is there no point at which they stop believing the shining mantle of their sheer good nature makes up for everything? Oh, not for them the bother and the effort of facing facts. No. All they do is let their terrible affection brim over on the ones they love, ignoring the fact that, without honesty, they might as well be spilling lava on them. Tirelessly these optimists haul up their buckets of excuses from what they claim to be a bottomless well of sympathy, even of sacrifice. 'I really didn't want to worry you.' 'I thought the last thing you needed was to have more on your plate.' 'I meant to tell you just as soon as everything had come out right.' Oh, saintly. Positively saintly! The trouble is, without plain dealing and your honour bright, such great and sheltering 'love' can end up hanging over the victim like a pall as in stroll the bailiffs. Lovers like these should pick their partners very carefully, or they might find themselves, not just thrown out but, worse, living with someone who has had enough of love and kisses, flowers and pretty meals on trays: someone now looking, not for Mr Perfect, but for one nugget of unshifting truth that can be used to take revenge.

The bastard. Sneaky bastard. What a shit!

9

I CAME HOME TO A HOUSE ABLAZE WITH LIGHT. A MAN IN A dark suit was in the kitchen, talking to Geoff. Minna was sobbing in her new boyfriend's arms and getting hysterical because she couldn't raise Harry on his mobile.

'What's going on?'

'It's Mum,' she wailed. 'Josh and I found her. She was wrapped in a blanket on the sofa. At first I thought that she was just asleep, and so we left her. But . . .'

Oh, brilliant! What great timing! I walk through the door, fizzing with outrage, all geared up to hurl her father into the street, and her damn mother's died! I could have *spat*. Instead I stood back, watching Geoff show his sober-suited visitor across the hall to the front door. As he passed Minna, the man cupped Frances's house keys more discreetly in his palm and said to Geoff in guarded tones, 'And you'll keep ringing your son? Every few minutes?'

I took it as a tactful way of saying, 'If your boy bumps into us, he'll get a shock.' And so he would, because although we'd been expecting Frances's death for months, it still seemed strange, as if that steady waiting had done no more than keep reminding us that Frances was dying, and not accustom us to Frances dead.

It was a long, long evening. Geoff couldn't read my face, and he said nothing when I went upstairs without a word. (I expect he thought I was leaving him to grieve with his family.) Josh was allowed to stay. I heard him pulling out the sofa bed, and, in the early hours, I heard his quiet footfalls up the stairs.

Anxiety stirred. I nudged Geoff. 'Time to start banging up and down the landing?'

He dredged himself from sleep. 'What do you mean?'

'A mercy fuck,' I warned. 'About to start next door.'

Indeed, the bed already had begun to creak, and Minna's quiet sobbing was stilling to occasional sniffs.

Geoff sounded irritable. 'It is her business, Tilly. She is eighteen.'

Maybe. But in my mind's eye I could plainly see the silver-backed sheet of pills that had tumbled from Minna's backpack on the Sunday before, blistered only till Wednesday.

'That bust-up with Arif was weeks ago. She may well not be up to speed on taking care.'

'A bit late now.'

'Not necessarily,' I said. 'I should have thought a father ambling up and down outside might well quell the urge. Or at the very least put the two of them into a more cautious frame of mind.'

Geoff pulled his pillow closer and punched it up again, ready to go back to sleep. 'I shouldn't have thought so, Tilly.' He gave the matter a moment's further thought. 'And it has been the shittiest day.'

'What are you saying, Geoff? "Whatever works"?'

He didn't deign to answer. His daughter, not mine. 'Well,' I said in a voice that brimmed with sarcasm, 'let's just hope one of the things that *isn't* working is her fertile body.'

He just pretended he'd gone back to sleep.

Over breakfast, I asked him, 'When will the funeral be? Is it decided?'

He looked washed out. 'Thursday, they think.' He gave me a pleading look over his mug of tea. 'You will be here on Thursday, won't you, Tilly? I don't believe I can do it without you.'

'Oh, I don't know,' I said. 'Look at it this way. You've managed to remortgage a flat and sell a whole house without my knowing a single thing about it. I should have thought that getting through a funeral would be a breeze.'

Maybe it *was* cruel. I still think he deserved it. The silence hung between us, then his head went down, his shoulders shook, and he was crying, not like a man but like a child. I'd never seen anything like it. Grown men cry often enough. There was an accident on one of our rigs a couple of years ago, and lots of the men wept. Pete and Anton had both been popular, and Anton had four small children. But that sort of crying was of the 'Don't mind me, these tears just keep leaking out' sort. Geoff's was extraordinary. He was blubbing like a five-year-old. Snot bubbled from his nose, the tears streamed, he had slug trails up his sleeves, and the noise he made was close to that frightful 'boo-hooing' you hear from toddlers.

'For God's sake!' I told him. 'Pull yourself together. Think of poor Minna. She can hear you upstairs.'

He just kept wailing. The phone rang. It was Harry. 'What's going *on*? Why are you leaving messages all over town? Mum *knew* that I was spending last night at Tod's flat. I *told* her I'd be—'

'Listen,' I interrupted him. 'It's good you didn't go home last night. There's been some really bad news.'

He knew at once. 'Can I please speak to Dad?' he said, cheering me mightily with the firm reminder of just how marginal I'd always been with this particular family – indeed, how little I'd be missed. I held the phone out to Geoff, then poked him to look up and notice. Wildly, he shook his head, but he did have the grace to quieten. I put the phone back to my ear. 'Your dad's upstairs with Minna,' I said to Harry. 'She's crying her eyes out and he's trying to comfort her.'

'Really? I thought I heard something.' There was a long, long pause. Then: 'Tilly, is Mum . . . ?' I heard him swallow hard. 'Is Mum . . . at home still?'

I took it carefully. 'I don't believe so, Harry. I rather think that they'll have taken her away to get things . . .' What was the bloody word? '. . . ready.'

'*Ready?*' There was a rush of anger. 'Like *what*? Like cut about on a *slab*?'

It was the Harry of childhood nightmares back again. 'Christ, no!' I told him firmly. 'There won't be any of that.'

'Promise?'

'I promise. The doctors already know everything they need.'

'I'm coming round.' Almost before he'd finished saying it, he had hung up.

Geoff lifted a head and said through blubbering slug trails, 'Is that true?'

'What?'

'About not having to have an autopsy?'

'How should I know?' I snapped. 'I don't know the first bloody thing about funerals. All I know is, that's what he needed to hear.' I made for the door. 'And if it isn't right, he won't find out till he's a bit less shocked.'

He called me back. 'See, Tilly? You tell lies too, when it suits you.'

I turned and stared. Was he trying to compare my easing a twenty-one-year-old through the first moments of shock after losing his mother with his own solid deceptions? '*What* did you say?' I asked in a tone deliberately shaded to scare him.

'Nothing.' His voice did tremble, and not just from leftover tears.

'Good,' I said icily, and assumed I wouldn't hear another word. But after a moment or two he was back on his hobby horse. (Really, the man was craven.)

'Tilly, you will come to the funeral, won't you? I know I can't manage without you.'

I took a moment to think. There was no way that I could

throw him out that night. Better to leave the whole sorry parting till after the service. Then I could easily persuade him to
move into Frances's house for 'just a few days' to see his son and
daughter through the first throes of grief. And I'd not have
him back. The perfect solution.

I didn't want him to suspect that I was stalling. So, to cover
my tracks, I drove a bargain. 'Promise you'll never lie to me
again?'

'Never. I swear, Til.'

What is the word of a liar worth? Fuck nothing. But I let it
go. 'And no leaving out the truth? No more weasel excuses: "I
didn't think you'd want to know" or "Didn't I mention it?" or
any of that crap?'

He blew his nose fruitily. 'No, no. I absolutely promise. I've
learned my lesson, Tilly. I'll do *anything* rather than lose you.'

Surely he couldn't think someone like me would cave in so
soon? The moment his wits returned, he'd realize that I was
playing for time and manage to thwart me. Desperate to get
through the next few days without having to wade through
washes of pleading and blubbering, I looked round for some
way of convincing him I was in earnest. 'All right, then. Write
your promise down.'

He stared.'What do you mean?'

'You know. Write down what you've just promised. "No
lies, no leaving information out, no sneaky little deceptions of
any sort. That is the deal." Then sign it.'

'Sign it?'

He looked offended, rather as if he took it poorly I had the nerve to question his good faith. You had to hand it to the man: he could snap out of denial, then back in again, in no time at all.

'Yes. *Sign* it.'

Shaking his head as if in wonder, he tore a square of paper from the shopping-list note block, and made enough of a labour of the writing task to make it clear he would have rolled his eyes if he had dared. In the end, handing it over, he asked me, 'And what are you going to do with this?'

I checked the wording, then I slid it into my pocket. 'Keep it, of course.'

'But *why*?'

'For when it happens again.'

'It isn't going to happen, Tilly. I'm a changed man. Believe me.'

I could have said, 'No, *you* believe *me*, Geoff. Nobody ever changes.' But Minna was coming down the stairs. And anyway I couldn't be bothered. What would have been the point?

The next few days were grim indeed. Harry vanished back to Tod's flat and all attempts to get him to respond to phone calls failed. Tod kept insisting Harry would show up for the funeral, and he was 'fine'. I had my doubts. The next time Geoff put the phone back on its cradle, shaking his head and shrugging, I said, 'You should go over there and root him out.'

'Do you think so?'

'I do. After all, Tod does have a reputation.'

'I never heard Frances saying anything about him.'

'I expect she had other things on her mind,' I told him tartly. 'Nonetheless, when Tod was back in school there was a lot of talk about him dabbling in drugs and stuff.'

Geoff was well back on form. Ignoring the times I'd warned him of his son's suspiciously elated moods, he said complacently, 'Oh, I think Harry's sensible enough not to get tangled up in anything like that.'

I rolled my eyes and muttered, 'If you say so, dear,' under my breath. I had enough to deal with anyway, managing Minna. Back in our house till after the funeral, one minute she'd be in a flood of tears and the next storming into the kitchen demanding to be allowed to deliver the eulogy.

'*You?*' I'd said, startled.

She shot me a very sullen look. 'Why not? Why shouldn't I be the one to talk about my own mother? I knew her best, after all.'

'Of course,' I soothed. 'I didn't mean you shouldn't. Not at all. I was just a little surprised.'

'I don't see why.'

'Well,' I defended myself, remembering all those times she couldn't choose an ice-cream, 'I suppose I just never thought of you as . . .'

Admittedly I faltered, not at all sure how to finish. But there was still no need for her to jump in so aggressively. 'Perhaps you haven't been looking.'

And perhaps I hadn't. The tall cold girl who stood there glowering was no one I recognized. Maybe in all those hours that she'd been slipping off to the Odeon when she should have been in school, she'd learned more than I thought. Dismissing me, she turned back to her father. 'I want to do it. So just say I can.'

'Sweetheart,' he told her, 'I'd be thrilled. And so would your mother have been.'

So that was that. Flashing a look of triumph at me as she passed, she flounced from the room. I don't know if she wrote the eulogy alone or if Josh helped. I know he was around an awful lot, and most of their time was spent in her bedroom. The evening before the funeral, he went off to borrow a dark jacket from a friend, and Minna came downstairs with four handwritten pages she handed to her father. 'What do you think?'

Geoff read them through, and hugged her. Determined not to be treated as if I were invisible under my own roof, I picked up the sheets of paper from the table one by one and read them myself. The only bit I didn't care for much was when she said 'and even Tilly came to love and respect her', but there was nothing to be done about that. 'Just grin and bear it,' I'd have told myself if grinning hadn't seemed so out of place. So I just bore it.

True to form, in the morning Harry failed to arrive at the agreed time.

Geoff shifted his weight from one foot to the other. 'Maybe he's gone straight there.'

'Perhaps he isn't coming.'

Geoff inspected his watch for the tenth time. 'The car can't wait much longer. We will have to go.'

'I'll pin a note on the back door, just in case,' I said. 'With money for a taxi.'

As soon as I stepped into the kitchen, I could see Harry's shadow on the ribbed glass. I opened the door. My Christ, the boy was in a state. The black tie I'd sent round was all awry. His hair was sticking up, his voice was slurred, and his jacket was coated with cat hairs.

I stood in silence for a moment while he stood swaying. Then I said, 'Ready to go?'

'Ready,' he said, then added insolently, 'I forgot to ask. Is this a fry-up? Or a dig-and-drop?'

I rammed him up against the wall, adding a graze on his cheek to his other scruffy aspects. 'Just knock it off, shit-head!'

He tried to pull himself together. 'Sorry, Til.' Out seeped the tears.

'That's all right,' I consoled him. 'No hard feelings, Harry. Just "time and place" and all that.' And, putting my arm around him, I led him through to join his sister and his weeping father.

The funeral was over by three, and not even Frances's mother stayed long at the reception. To be free of the stragglers – mostly a gang of grimly positive women from Frances's self-help group – I led the way to a bar. It was a dismal couple of hours. I didn't drink. Harry was scowling, and Minna kept going on and on about how very much her mother must have enjoyed 'looking down on us saying such nice things'. I glanced at Josh, wondering if this sort of sentimental drivelling would put an end to the relationship once and for all, but he kept nodding encouragement. For God's sake! Did the boy not have a forkful of brain? Or was he one of those lovers who simply buy the whole package, however daffy, until things end? Minna kept turning to her father and squeezing his hand. 'And *you*,' she rebuked him at one point with wet eyes, 'you should have let me put in that bit about how *kind* you were to Mum.' I didn't miss Geoff's slightly panicked look, and the small frown as he pressed her knee to silence her. I simply waited. I had never known the man get through more than one pint without a trip to the Gents and, sure enough, as soon as the conversation moved back once more to Josh's idyllic childhood in Cornwall, Geoff took his chance. 'Won't be a moment.'

The instant he was out of earshot, I moved in. Nodding at Geoff's departing back, I interrupted Josh to say to Minna, 'He *was* good to your mother, wasn't he?'

She couldn't wait to draw us all back into her little family love-fest. 'Yes, he was. Right to the end. And very generous.'

'Very,' I encouraged her.

'And Mum appreciated that. In fact, she said she'd *never* have been able to carry on with everything without his help.'

At first I took her to be referring to Frances's last frail return to the house, and the times she'd needed help with the wheel-chair. But Minna kept on with her praises. 'I mean, I know Dad doesn't even believe in crystals and homeopathy and reiki and all that other stuff. And it was horribly expensive, especially with everyone having to come to the house. Mum said she'd never have been able to afford it herself. Never. And even after Terence told him it was a waste of money, Dad kept on helping her.'

'Well, there's your father for you. Generous to a *fault*.'

I tried not to spit out the last word, and hoped that the sound of my chair legs scraping back over the tiles would disguise at least some of the venom. I marched off for my coat. When Geoff came back from the lavatory, we left at once. Harry insisted on being dropped off at Tod's flat. The rest of us went home. Even before Geoff had reached the drinks cabinet, Minna and Josh had vanished upstairs. It wasn't long before, down through the ceiling, we could make out a sort of rhythmic reprise of the bed creakings of a few nights earlier. I wondered if Minna was quite so confident now that her mother was 'looking down' on her with such great pleasure. But I said nothing and just followed up the stairs a short while later.

Geoff caught me coming down again with my bag. 'You're not *off*? Not *tonight*?'

I checked my watch in self-important fashion. 'I'm sorry it's so rushed. I hadn't realized how long everything would take. They'll all be waiting.'

'Waiting?'

'At the hotel,' I lied. 'The rest of the team have been there all day, preparing for tomorrow.'

'What's tomorrow?'

'I told you,' I said glibly. 'We're training university recruiters. It's been arranged for months. The presentations go on all weekend, and then I'm straight up north.'

145

'But—'

'Listen,' I told him, 'I'll give you a ring in the morning. But right now I am keeping people waiting.'

Beaten, he stepped back.

I pecked him on the cheek. 'Chin up. Look after Minna.'

I don't think I've ever driven quite so fast over the speed bump at the end of our street. I made straight for the bypass. A few miles up, I stopped at The Danesmoor Inn. They had a room and, within half an hour, I was in the bath, breathing more easily and reading the paper, and waiting for the knock on the door that meant room service had at last arrived with my large whisky in a nice clean glass.

Talk about needy. I hardly seemed to get through a day without one of his phone calls. 'Not coming home *again*? But, Tilly, it'll be over a week!'

'I'm sorry, Geoff. We're having a hell of a time getting the shims under these derrick footings.' I missed his next moan when the generator I was leaning against sprang back to life. 'Look, I'll be home when I can. This is a big unit we're moving, and there are problems with the pinion gear teeth.'

I flapped a hand at the rest of the team, who were already rolling their eyes, making faces and sniggering.

'Well, hurry home when you can,' Geoff pleaded. 'I'm feeling crap here. Harry's disappeared again. He won't return my calls. And Minna's going down to Torbury Bay.'

'Torbury Bay?'

'Cornwall. To meet Josh's family. So I'll be all alone.'

The tone of self-pity galvanized me into spite. 'Why don't you do something useful while she's gone? Surprise her. Paint her bedroom. Tart up the kitchen. Put back that side of the porch Frances had to take down to park her wheelchair.'

'Oh, *that* house. There's no point really. After all, the lease will end in June.'

Can people sense when I turn dangerous? For it did seem to me that suddenly all the men had stopped their fooling and had fallen silent.

'Lease? I thought that Frances got the house when you divorced.'

'She did. But all those treatments . . . And the trip to Arizona, of course . . . This last place was a rental. Didn't you realize?'

He must have known from the silence that this was news. I suppose he was waiting. Presumably he thought we'd run through the old, old performance: 'You never told me.' 'Well, I thought you knew.' He may even have been a step ahead, waiting for me to say 'You *promised* me!' so he could argue triumphantly, 'No, Tilly. This doesn't count. Frances had sold her last house long before you made me sign that piece of paper.'

Instead, I held the phone out to the wind. 'Fixed pins in!' I yelled. 'Yoke pins to Out!'

It was a little skit we ran through each time Digger's wife phoned up in tears. The man could only take so much, then he would rouse everyone standing round into performance to help him get away.

'Raise yokes!'

They all came in on cue. 'Disengaged fore!'

'Yokes down!'

'Disengaged aft! Check pins!'

'Checked!' I held the phone down close to the generator and kicked its tin side so hard I must have deafened him.

'Raise yokes!' I yelled again. 'Disengage!'

'Disengaged!'

'Yokes up!'

I brought the phone back to my ear. 'Sorry, Geoff. Got to go. These bloody rack and pinion gears are playing up again.'

I couldn't even tell if we'd impressed him. I'd rung off.

10

BACK TO SQUARE ONE, AND SOL'S PLAN TO GET GEOFFREY ON HIS feet again before planting the boot on his backside. I started nagging Sol to look at Print-It! The first I heard that he was actually getting on with it was when Geoff told me Doris had begun complaining about some old geezer who sat for hours on the window ledge, claiming it was where he'd arranged to 'meet his wife'. Doris was outraged that he'd even asked to use the lavatory, and, on his way out, stumbled through not just both storerooms, but also the little kitchen overlooking the back yard.

'She calls you an old geezer,' I told Sol next time we spoke.

Mightily put out, he said, 'That isn't *me*. I haven't time to prowl around failing businesses. That's Mr Stassinopolous, looking for a berth for his son.'

'What does he think?'

'Same as me. Prime site. One could make something of it. Have you spoken to Geoff?'

'He's banking on you.'

Clearly Sol and this Mr Stassinopolous had been discussing the terms. 'A clear-cut take-over of the lease? A token payment for the stuff in the storerooms and simple transfer of all the equipment guarantees and rentals?'

'He's over a barrel, Sol. Now it's all over, Geoff just wants to get out.'

And out he was. Within a couple of months, the deal was struck. Geoff handed over to the Stassinopolous boy, and came home pleased as punch, as if the deal had been a master-stroke of business acumen and not the end of his financial hopes. 'He is a nice young man. Very pleasant, with a most charming wife.' He was nodding in self-important fashion, as if to stress his feelings of satisfaction. 'Naturally I asked him, as a favour to me, to keep Mrs Mackie and Doris on the books.'

I looked up from my estimations of fixed load. 'Refresh my memory, Geoff. Why would the Stassinopolous boy owe you a favour?'

Geoff looked a bit put out. 'Well, he has done rather well for himself, hasn't he, getting Print-It!'

'Thanks to his father.'

Geoff turned his back. 'No need to be unpleasant, Tilly. I've left things ship-shape. He's a fortunate boy. I reckon he owes me a favour and I think he knows it.'

'Oh, yes? Watch this space.'

Indeed, within a month, both women were gone. George Stassinopolous paid them cash for a week or two while he was picking their brains, then waved them goodbye. Next time I glanced in the shop, it seemed to be staffed with students, the window was plastered with special offers, and, for the first time ever, the place appeared to be humming.

Meanwhile, Geoff took his time, looking for work. Every few days, when I prompted, he'd say in lordly fashion, 'I'm just asking around a bit,' as if he'd spent his life hobnobbing with useful business contacts instead of being a rather stay-at-home bloke, happy to go for days on end speaking mostly to food-shop assistants and to his own employees.

'Why don't you phone that firm who used to drop off your paper and stuff?' I suggested one morning.

'Stationery Supplies?' Geoff looked quite pleased. 'Excellent idea, Til. I should have thought of that myself.'

I made the mistake of warming to the notion. 'As I recall, you were forever going on about how hard it was for them to find a reliable driver.'

'Driver?'

His beady look annoyed me. 'Well, what did you think? That, with your track record, they'd invite you to sit on the board?'

He turned back to his paper. 'I'm sure you don't mean to be horrid, Til.'

Don't say a word, I told myself. It's not your problem. There's no need to rise to the bait. You can get through this without pointing out that you're right and he's wrong. And Geoff is bound to find a job. Employers are supposed to spend their waking hours scouring the land for clean and literate people.

That gave me another idea. 'Have you tried going down the Job Centre?'

If I'd said 'Have you tried selling your sperm?' he couldn't have acted more startled. 'Sorry, Til?'

'The Job Centre,' I repeated. 'Have you been down there? Have you signed on and given them your details?'

'No, I haven't!'

He was quite short with me. I left the room, thinking I'd give him a couple more days. Surely the idea would sink in that he was going to have to junk his lofty so-called 'management skills', and get a real job. Failing that, I planned to put Sol's plan in moth-balls and kick him out anyway, pitiless as it might appear to him and to others. I was halfway up the stairs when the phone rang. Hoping it might be some stab at employment in the offing, I stayed on the landing to listen. It was a little hard to make out what was going on at the other end. All I could hear from Geoff were broken-off phrases: 'No, Harry—' 'Slow *down*. I can't fol-low—' 'Start *again*, Harry.' 'How can—?' 'Please, Harry! Stop!'

It sounded so desperate that I leaned over the banister. Spotting me standing there, Geoff frantically signalled me through to the bedroom to pick up the extension. He was still trying to calm his son: 'Take it easy, Harry. Try to expl—' 'Harry, I can't make sense of—'

I picked up the phone. If Geoff hadn't made it clear that it was Harry, I'm not sure I'd have guessed. The voice was strung out and hysterical. The words were spat out at machine-gun speed. The venom in the voice was horrible. It was a hate call and the object of the hate was me.

'See, Dad? Did you hear that click? She's picked up one of
the phones. She's listening! She listens to everything, Tilly
does. She—'

'Harry, this is ridic—'

'You don't know what she's like. You think she's nice, but
she's not. She's actually *dangerous*. She can send voices into
people's brains to stop them thinking their own thoughts. She
can—'

I put the phone down. Bloody, bloody drugs! Wouldn't you
know it? Just as the moment arrives to make a break for it, here
comes the son to join the needy father. I flung the wardrobe
doors wide. There were my trusty matching carry bags. There
were my clothes. My toiletries were standing in a row, just
waiting to be tipped into their daisy-lined holder. Just make a
run for it, I told myself. Leave Geoff in this stupid house for
now. Let him get on with it, and pay a solicitor to winkle him
out later. Anything – *anything* – rather than have more of your
life chewed up by these endless delays and your own indecision.
Quick! Take your chance, Til. Bugger off. Then you can live
alone.

Alone! Even the word sounded magical. To think and feel
only as I chose. Be answerable to no one, feel guilty about
nothing, live my own life and feel time my own again. It would
be like a *gift*. Manna from heaven. But even as I was hurling
the first clothes into the bag, there came a swipe of real shame.
There you go, whispered the part of me that wasn't quite tough
enough. There you go, drizzling your petty discontents over
everything, and putting your grievances above the problems of

a damaged boy. For a moment I froze, my folded jeans in my hand. But then I tossed them into one of the bags as planned. After all, who had let this problem arise in the first place? Who was it who had allowed his son – against clearly stated advice – to spend the most testing week of his young life in a flat with a druggie? What had Geoff *thought* would happen, for Christ's sake? Did he assume that Tod would sit on his bean-bag, puffing away on prime spliffs, and good old Harry would be waving away each offer of blissful oblivion with some namby-pamby, wholesome 'No, thanks. I think I'll have a cup of tea'? The stupid, *stupid* man, forever allowing his problems to breed out of sheer bloody idleness.

Furious again, I hurled the things I couldn't do without, one after another, into the bags on the bed. Geoff was a lazy shit. He was a selfish bastard. I'd warned him again and again. Now let him reap what he himself had sown. Was it *my* job to stick around to help him pick up the pieces? For heaven's sake! It wasn't as if I'd been put on the planet to sort out things for Geoffrey Anderson. It was time he learned to clear up his own messes. They were his children, after all, not mine. In went the clock and the toiletries. In went the things I needed from my top drawer. Was it my fault that, when the letter came from my solicitor asking him to leave, he wouldn't even have a home to offer his son and his daughter? No, it was not. It was because he hadn't ever made the effort to learn the very first thing about himself, and coming to terms with all your own limitations is the most basic part of growing up. If tens of thousands of little girls can face the fact they'll never be ballerinas, never have a horse of their own to adore, never strut down a catwalk to a chorus of gasps, what is so wrong with one man coming to realize he doesn't have the skills to run a shop? You can't forever be throwing things away, then piteously looking round for someone else to bail you out. Was it my fault he'd tossed half his savings down the drain to help a woman waste money on crystals and weird therapies and a whole host of other crap peddled to people so scared of dying they've taken leave of their senses? Bad enough that he hadn't dared tell me. But surely even Geoffrey could have summoned the guts to try to stop Frances. Terence had tried. He'd even written a letter to try to get Geoff to support him. Perhaps if the two of them had managed to hold firm then, come the end of June, Harry and Minna might still have had a roof of their own over their heads instead of becoming even more dependent on mine.

Grim thought. I forced the last of my computer stuff into the bag. The phone call with Harry couldn't last for ever, however loopy the lad had become. Geoff would be up the stairs soon, to report. I wanted to slide out before the tears, before the argument. I simply wanted to be gone. I knew what everyone else would think. I didn't have to wonder for a moment what my brother would say when I told him I'd scarpered. 'Oh, come on, Til. So Geoff let a few things slide. Give the poor man a break. It's only because he's so taken up with spoiling you that he never bothers with other things. As for his secrets, don't forget he hides the truth just as much from himself. Let the poor sod off the hook, Til. You're no picnic to live with either. So go back home.'

No, I thought. Not this time. No one will persuade me back. Not Ed. Not Donald. Not even the blokes in the office or on the rig. I'll have no more of men sticking together to support their own crappy standards. Ed had been quick enough to make it clear he didn't want to risk his own share of my mother's money or easy way of life. What had he said? 'No worries, Til. He won't get a bean out of me. I'll be as hard as nails.' So now, his shade could not cajole me into some softer path to take myself. No, I was off. And slinging the computer case over my shoulder, I reached down for the travel bags.

And felt the whole house shake. Downstairs, the front door slammed. I could hear footsteps hurrying down the path and I crossed to the window. My car was blocking Geoff's, and, without even glancing up, he started sorting through his bunch of keys to find my spare. I struggled with the window latch as I banged on the glass. 'Hey! Take your own car! I need mine. Hang on a moment till—'

But even before I'd managed to make myself heard, Geoffrey had thrown himself into the driving seat, slammed shut the car door and sped away.

Leaving me with a twelve-year-old hatchback with a rusty floor, a boot that won't open and a temperamental starter. I sank down on the bed. How many times in a row could my determination to get away be derailed by this family? Come *on*, I urged myself. Make a break for it. A car counts for nothing. Take a taxi if you must. Or, just for now, drive off in his bloody heap.

But just the fact that I'd been left with a car I couldn't depend on drained a lot of my fury away. After all, whose fault was that? Mine. Mine alone. I'd promised to fix the sodding starter motor weeks ago, and never bothered. Geoff, on the other hand, would never have put off doing that sort of favour for me. He was a generous-spirited soul who held me so dear that things he could do for me always came top of his list. At heart, let's face it, how you judge a man depends on what you value and what you want. If what I wanted was love, Geoff offered it in spades.

He always had.

And me? A different story. Here came the moment when he'd lost his children's mother, his savings, even his job. To cap it all, his grieving son had stuffed enough drugs down his neck to float full-blown psychosis. And what was I doing? After years and years of eating the meals he'd cooked, driving the car he'd washed and sleeping in beds he'd changed, I was lifting my travel bags, to get away.

I put my head in my hands, defeated yet again. This man was dashing out into the night because he loved his son. Maybe it was a stupid way to spend his energies, slamming stable doors after horses had bolted. But that was Geoff. And everyone else loved him all the more dearly for it. The mother of his children accepted his well-meant help right to the end. His daughter's eyes filled with tears at the mere thought of him. Even his son's first concern in paranoia appeared to be the safety of his father.

They were all round me now, shaking their fingers. I could

see them. Harry and Minna. Ed and my mother. Donald and guys from the rigs. I could as good as hear their voices, stern and implacable. And every one of them was saying the same thing. 'Shame on you, Tilly Foster. Shame on you. Unpack that bag at once.'

And so I did.

I was still in the most chastened of moods when, early next morning, Minna came round from the other house. 'Where is Dad?'

Unable to face the fuss I knew would follow if I admitted he was at the hospital, talking to doctors, I stalled. 'Oh, just off out.'

I thought at first she might have come to look for her brother. But clearly his absence overnight was nothing to remark on – at least not to me – because she made herself a cup of herbal tea and spent a good couple of minutes fiddling with pieces of starter motor laid out on the table before taking a deep breath and saying, 'Tilly, I'm pregnant. I just did one of those tests and the blue line came up at once. What shall I *do*?'

I felt too weak after a sleepless night to offer anything much. 'What do you *feel* like doing?'

Unthinkingly, she slid her arms around her belly, making the answer pretty obvious, and so I said, 'If you're in doubt, Minna, you should certainly think about keeping it.'

This clearly wasn't what she was expecting from me. 'Really? Is that what you'd do?'

'No,' I admitted.

'But you think *I* should?'

'I can't say, can I, sweetheart? It's your decision. You're eighteen.'

'*Nine*teen. But what about Dad?'

I shrugged. 'This is a matter between you and Josh.'

She made a face. 'Josh says he wants to get married. He says he's wanted to get married right along.' She sighed. 'But I'm not sure. I mean, what happens when he tells his mum? She's going to *kill* us.'

It must be odd to be so young that you can let such huge decisions spin on such foolish things. Maybe it was because her brother had insisted I was 'dangerous' that I was determined not to let a single destructive comment escape my lips. 'His mum will do the same as every other mother – give him a right royal bollocking, scowl at the two of you for several months, then fall in love with the baby.'

Minna looked thrilled. 'You think so?'

'I do.' I had another poke around the part of the motor that was proving most tricky. 'And look at it this way, if she doesn't soften, you can always console yourself that she wouldn't have been any great loss to your new family.'

'New family . . .' Yet again, the tell-tale arms slid round her stomach. 'Weird idea!'

'Well,' I warned, 'don't get too taken up with it before giving a tiny bit of thought to the other.'

'The other?'

'Getting rid of it.'

'Oh, no! I couldn't.' She appeared quite shocked.

So that was that. The baby's fate was settled in the length of time it takes a girl to drink one Apple Passion. Minna went straight to the hospital to tell her father. ('He *cried*, Til. He burst into tears and said, if we were pleased, then he'd be *mad* not to be pleased for us.') Next day, she went again, to visit her brother. ('It's *awful*, Tilly. He's laid out like a zombie with his face all stiff. And he smells funny.') Then she was gone, down with the marriage-minded Josh to face his family in Cornwall. No worries there, it seemed. They took to her right from the start. Grandma Elise in particular, Josh reported when they came back, was taken with her sweet nature and let it be known that there would always be a home for the young family in one of the 'barns' that stood on her ancient farm. Brushing the compliment aside, Minna took up the story. 'You should *see* it, Tilly. Call it a barn? It's *fabulous*. It has these great black beams, and pretty rooms with tiny pointy windows, and you can see the sea. Oh, and the kitchen's a huge wide space with lovely blue tiling and a massive old cooking range that Elise moved from the big house. And in the garden there are apple trees and dog roses all over. And—'

I watched Geoff's face as it fell, and took it upon myself to interrupt Minna's parade of bliss. 'So you are tempted, then?'

She suddenly realized how it must have sounded. 'We-ell,' she said with a shy glance at Josh, 'not while poor Harry's so ill. I wouldn't like to be so far away from him that I couldn't visit.'

But that didn't last for long. And fair enough. After all, sitting for hours with a brother who barely speaks to you can swiftly pall. 'I can't keep going there, Dad. Not if he's going to smoke at me all the time.'

'He's not smoking *at* you, sweetie. It's just that smoking's all that any of them in there can do to pass the time, and so they do it.'

'He could read. Or play his guitar, or something.'

'Minna, his concentration's shot to hell. And have you looked at his hands? They're shaking.'

After the next visit, she was even more incensed. 'Dad, he won't even *compromise*. It took me ages to get there, it's so out of the way. And then Harry couldn't even be bothered to come down with me in the lift so we could be outside while he was smoking, so I just spent most of the time outside in the corridor. What's the point of that?'

'That's just the way your brother is at the moment, Minna. He will get better, honestly.'

'Perhaps he will. But we have to think of our *baby*.'

And Josh was right behind her. I could tell from the bland expression on his face that this conversation had been planned. I turned to Geoff. His hair was sticking up on end from running his hands through, and I saw his eyes fall on the whisky bottle on the sideboard.

Things seemed quite desperate, so I made a family decision. 'Why don't you take a break?' I said to Minna and Josh. 'We can cope here. Why don't you two go and spend a bit of time with Josh's family. It'll do you good, and you can stop worrying about the baby.'

Could she have sounded more hopeful? 'What, like a few weeks, even?'

Geoff looked a bit startled, but I said, 'Why not? Your

brother's so inside himself, he doesn't get much joy from anyone's visits. Perhaps you should save your energies for when they'll do more good.'

'Really?' She looked as if she could have hugged me. Then she turned to her father. 'Dad? Is that all right with you? You don't mind if we go down to Torbury Bay and live in the barn for a while?'

He'd reached that stage when he would have sold his soul to anyone for one stiff drink. 'No, really. Tilly's right. You're probably better off away from the whole bloody boiling for a while. It's best you think of the baby. You go down to Cornwall. We can manage here.'

Her arms were round him. 'Thank you, Dad! Thank you.'

Clearly, she'd got her heart's desire. And who can blame her for not wanting to spoil her growing happiness by hanging round a hospital ward? The sheer disabling misery of the place chewed its way even into Geoff, who set off each day hoping to see some small improvement in his son, and came home detailing endless attempts to talk in private to impatient, seen-it-all staff, and trying to put out of his mind Harry's demented diatribes and extraordinary claims about insects crawling under his skin, and men watching from rooftops.

'At least you're not the only enemy,' Geoff used to tell me, dropping his coat on the hall chair and making straight for the bottle standing waiting on the sideboard.

'Oh, ho,' I said. 'The man with the spyglass today again, was it?'

'Mostly.' He took a slug. (There was no other way of describing it. Half the glass went in one go.) Geoff refilled the tumbler before he even bothered to turn round. 'But not before we'd had another of those fugues on the Tilly people.'

That's what we called them. Harry had formed the view (just like my mother) that there were two of me. But whereas my mother had only ever felt a mild shade of resentment for the 'stand offish' one who parked herself on the windowseat to skim through the papers, Harry kept coming back to the full-blown belief that there were actually two separate people who lived with his father: Good Tilly and Bad Tilly. 'It makes me sound like something out of a children's book,' I complained to Geoff. 'Bad Tilly breaking all the toys and Good Tilly trying to stop her.' He'd only wince. The grim reality of dealing with the mad wipes out that part of you that's open even to registering a light-hearted comment, let alone responding in kind. At first, I'd offered to do a share of the visiting; but since my presence only seemed to fire up Harry, I soon fell back on being useful boning up on side-effects, and the tiresome legalities surrounding those who firmly believe the medication offered them is some new poison smuggled in by men who are watching its debilitating effects through binoculars from rooftops.

And getting away – to the shore office, to the rigs, even to Mother, now grey and soundless in her own hospital bed. Anything was preferable to being at home. So it was purely by chance that, on the morning Minna rang, I was the only one there.

It was the old, unthinking greeting. 'Oh. Hi, Tilly. I

thought you'd be away in Aberdeen.'

'I take it you want Geoff.'

My chilly briskness threw her only for a moment. She pressed on hurriedly. 'Is he about?'

'I'm afraid he's already left for the hospital.'

'Damn!' Her frustration obvious, she did the best job she could of switching to sisterly concern. 'So how *is* Harry?'

'Not so brilliant.' I would have carried on and told her more, but clearly she couldn't resist the chance to twist the conversation as fast as she could back to her own concerns. 'Well, that's really what I wanted to know. Because everyone down here thinks that, what with the baby on the way and all that, it might be better all round if . . .'

'If . . . ?'

'If Josh and I got married.'

What can you say? 'I'm quite delighted for you, Minna. And so will your dad be, I'm sure.'

'Ye-es.' She sounded uneasy. 'Well, the thing is, Tilly, everyone down here thinks it might be nice to do it quite soon.'

'Quite soon?'

'Well, as soon as possible, really.'

Before she could no longer fit in the dress of her dreams, presumably. Before it was too late to be able to trail the words 'The baby was rather premature' in front of the neighbours later.

I wasn't going to help her out. 'I'm not sure, Minna. You see, what with things as they are' – I swear I put only the slightest tinge of mockery into the next two words – ' " up here" at the moment—'

She pounced so eagerly I knew that 'everyone down there' must already have things planned. 'Well, that's the point, really, Tilly. You see, Natalie and Caspar, and Elise – and Josh's sisters – and Josh as well, of course—'

'Pretty well everyone "down there", in fact.'

Did she even notice the mimicry? I don't believe she did.

'Yes. Everyone down here thinks that it might be easier if . . .'

She did at least have the grace to hesitate. And since I wanted to be able to make it clear to Geoff that there had been no possibility of his daughter having misunderstood the way things were 'up here', I made a point of interrupting to voice plain facts. 'The thing is, Minna, your brother certainly isn't well enough to travel. And, given the state Harry's in, your father certainly won't want to leave him.'

Again that eagerness. 'Well, that's the point, isn't it? Everyone down here thinks it might be best for me and Josh to have the simplest of weddings now, even without my side of the family, and then maybe another celebration up there when everyone's feeling more up to it.'

'You realize that could be quite a while?'

Her relief was evident. 'Oh, well. Never mind. We don't have to worry about that now, do we?'

I lost my patience. 'Well,' I said, 'so long as everyone *down there* is perfectly happy.' And then, to stop her saying anything else that might annoy me, I said down the phone, 'Hello? Hello? Oh, damn this telephone! It's always cutting out.'

And I hung up.

165

*

But day by day, things with Harry did improve a bit. Each drug they tried took hold in less upsetting ways. The worst of the battiness passed. (And certainly, if Good and Bad Tilly were still in the forefront of Harry's mind, his father said much less about them.) Soon Harry was allowed the privilege of visits home, and Geoff would fetch him on the days I was away. The closeness of the timings – me barely out of the house before Harry was in it – could scarcely fail to irritate me with their reminder of the end of my marriage; but it was still a while before real resentment crept in. One night, instead of reaching forward as usual to take my coat as I walked into the house, Geoff stepped outside, forcing me into retreat, and pulled the door closed behind him. 'You told me sevenish,' he said, almost accusingly. 'Or even later.'

I was cold, I was tired, and in no mood to indulge Geoff and his family. 'So?'

'So Harry's still here.'

I shot him an evil look. 'This is my house, you know.'

'I know. It's just . . .'

'Just . . . ?'

Defeated, he stepped back and let me pass. I dropped my bag in the hall. Was this the moment to explain the only reason we were still together was Harry's illness and the sheer impossibility of throwing the pair of them out in the storm? But just then Harry appeared in the kitchen doorway and even managed a slightly sheepish 'Oh, hello there, Tilly,' before his father swept him safely away. I vanished up the stairs, forcibly reminding myself that Geoff was trapped inside this nightmare, while I, at least, did have the sheer relief of getting away. And get away I did, the very next morning with Donald's help, sandwiching someone else's unwanted trip to a troublesome semi-submersible between a trip to Mother in the hospital and a refresher course for safety skills I hadn't yet had time to lose. So it was scarcely surprising that, when a few wedding photos finally arrived from Minna, Geoff asked so tentatively, 'Shall I post them up to Aberdeen?'

'No, no,' I told him, suddenly curious. 'Something's been cancelled, so I'm coming home.'

What had I said? 'So long as everyone down there is perfectly happy'? Well, perfectly happy they did seem to be. For the simplest of weddings, it looked pretty fancy. I pored over the very few photographs Minna had dared send up to us (the perfunctorily mothballed guests), pointing out clues to the nature of the occasion. 'Everyone looks very dressed up. And isn't that a yew-lined path?' I glanced at Geoff. 'Did you know the ceremony was to be in church?'

Geoff didn't answer. He, too, had fallen into private-detective mode. 'That's bloody thick canvass for "a tiny marquee in case it rains".' He held the print closer. 'Tilly, this photo's grainier than the others. I reckon someone's cut half of it off, and tried to disguise it by getting what's left enlarged.'

I took it from him. 'They're hiding the wedding cake.' I pointed. 'See? Right at the edge there. That tiny rim of white.'

'You think that's icing?'

'I'll bet it is. And see where Minna's looking? If it's at the top of the cake, the bloody thing must have been the height of Mount Everest.'

Depressed enough for suspicion to have taken full hold, Geoff stabbed the next print with a finger. 'Why would there be a silver gravy boat on the edge of this table if it was all just sandwiches like she said?'

I passed him the next one. 'Look, here's another give-away. I take it she couldn't resist sending us this one so that we can join her in admiring the wonderful Elise—'

'Saint Elise of the Free Barn.'

'But see that puff of pink just behind?' He squinted where my finger rested. 'I reckon that's a bit of bridesmaid.' I put the boot in. 'And there *were* proper speeches – unless this bloke simply stood up to fart.'

Geoff pushed the photographs away and made a stab at humour. 'Good thing we didn't go. Her father-in-law's new suit would have put mine to shame.'

I didn't answer since it seemed so cruel to remind him we hadn't been invited. And I felt equally forlorn. That very morning I had looked at the calendar and noticed it was four months to the day since I had packed my bags. Four months of Harry so unhinged he made no sense. Four months of biding my time. And what had happened? Here, right at the end, as if to snuff out not just her father's hopes and dreams but also mine, came Minna, carelessly tossing the two of us out in the same basket. For, for the first time ever, Geoffrey and I had been cast out together: a fully equal pair.

And what did I feel? Disappointment, pure and hard – as if an almost certain passport to freedom had been snatched away at the last hour. Once more I would be forced by circumstance either to whistle as I packed my bags the moment Harry came back to his senses – cruel and hard-hearted Tilly –

Or look for yet another excuse to leave.

11

HARRY MADE PROGRESS. THOSE WHO HAVE BEEN THROUGH THIS particular wringer will know how time and again, and even in retreat, this sort of illness snatches back the days of hope till everyone involved is quite as raw and limp as in the worst times. But as the drug dosage lessened, Harry's weepiness subsided and his concentration began to return. Soon, even his hands stopped shaking, and he was pretty well back to his old self. 'A most optimistic prognosis,' one of the doctors admitted cheeringly. 'This could turn out to be a one-off, if he's lucky.'

'And if he stays away from all that crap that set it off in the first place,' I said tartly to Geoffrey, ripping his neatly written *Tod rang* off the telephone message pad and dropping it straight in the bin. A few days later, Harry came back from an appointment with the specialist and thundered up the stairs to the small room I'd recolonized since he moved back where Minna used to be. 'Tilly, where's Dad?'

'Carlisle. Some of that paper he delivered yesterday turned out to be the wrong sort.' I looked up from the installation sheet I was studying. 'Why? Everything all right?'

'Better than all right. That hospital bloke just said he doesn't want to see me again. I'm to make one last appointment with my regular doctor, and then I'm free.'

'Really? You mean, not just off their outpatient list, but really free not to go back for more check-ups?'

'What he said was, "See how it goes. Let's just give it a whirl."' True to the specialist's word, Harry stepped in the room to seize the back of my swivel chair and give it a celebratory spin. He took the first appointment that they offered him, a cancellation on the very next day, and came back on cloud nine. 'Tilly, she's wonderful! *Wonderful.*'

'Yes. Geoff said she was good when he—'

'No, not her. Not the doctor. Tara! The girl who's helping out for a few weeks in the dispensary.'

I stared at his soppy, smiling face. 'I hope for your sake she was just as smitten with you.'

'I made her laugh,' he said, the same way I'd have said 'I built a rocket' or 'I went to Mars', and launched into the story he told again to his father over supper, and then a third time after that, about helping this beautiful young woman shift a few boxes filled with patients' case notes taken out of the old cabinets across to the glossy new filing units she had arranged to be delivered. One of the doctors had stepped in the room and, seeing a stranger with armfuls of confidential records, asked sharply, 'What are you doing?'

ANNE FINE

'Oh, don't mind me,' it seems that Harry had responded airily. 'I'm just helping out with a cabinet reshuffle.'

Small enough joke. But it was Harry all over – the old Harry back again – and Geoffrey was thrilled. So he was predisposed right from the start to take to Tara. And take to her he did. When I came back from Aberdeen the following week, he told me excitedly, 'I've met her, Til! We all went out for pizza. I liked her enormously, and you can tell she's going to be so good for Harry.'

Perhaps, with things as they were, it wasn't surprising I felt the need to remind him that women aren't put on earth simply to serve some useful purpose for men. 'That's as may be. But what's she *like*?'

He scoured his brain for some way of describing her. Then out it came. 'She's very pretty and she's very nice.'

'Is that it?'

You could tell from the look on his face he realized he'd failed some test that left him baffled. So he thought some more. 'Oh, yes! And she's a Christian.'

'Meaning, exactly?'

'You know. She actually prays. And attends special church meetings and things. Oh, and when she opened her handbag, I saw a badge pinned on the inside flap.'

'A badge?'

'Yes. In the shape of a dove. It said, *I am a Christian, clean and clear.*'

'Curtains for Tod and the druggies, then. If it lasts . . .'

It lasted. No one could slide a sheet of paper between the

two of them all through the summer. Tara wasn't just pretty and Christian, she was bossy too. In the short time she worked in the dispensary, it seems she changed not just the cabinets but the computer procedures, the appointments system, and most of the doctors' schedules. 'My Christ, they'll be relieved when she goes back down south,' I whispered to Geoffrey after an hour of hearing Harry sing his girlfriend's praises. 'And I can't understand why she is going back to Business School when, left to herself, she could already run the whole bloody planet.'

'Her first degree isn't enough. She wants to get her Masters.'

'God help poor Harry,' I muttered, though it was plain that he was blooming under the strict new regime. His hours of wakefulness snapped back to being those of normal people. He shyly crossed the name of his usual sticky cereal off our shopping list and asked for crunchy granola. One day I even caught him reading a book. By the start of September, he was firmly back on track with his studies. I took him to be one of Tara's little projects – something to pass the time before her new course began. But I was wrong. It seemed the three-year age gap was of no significance to either, and Harry's plans for a little break from his studies in the middle of term suddenly included a trip down to Sussex.

'It's to meet Tara's mother,' Geoff explained.

I grinned. 'A-*ha*? The smoking widow?'

Geoff glanced round nervously. 'Don't say that, Tilly. It really isn't funny. This problem with the circulation in Gloria's legs is getting worse, and really worrying Tara.'

My sweet pink *arse*. As far as I could tell, Tara was simply peeved that her mother wasn't following her regular strictures about the evils of smoking with the same bovine keenness Harry had shown to kiss the rod of good health. My stepson was reduced to the odd snatched cigarette and lashings of toothpaste. What did I care? Each week that passed, he was a stronger, fitter and a happier person. Even his new beloved's organizational skills seemed to be brushing off on him. One day I found him at the kitchen table, poring over a map.

'Where's Torbury Bay, Til?'

I laid my finger on the little coastal haven into which Minna had vanished.

'It's not so far away from Sussex, then.'

'No. Only five counties and about two hundred miles.'

He missed the sarcasm. 'So Tara's right. We might as well arrange to visit while we're down there anyway.'

Thinking of all the times Geoff's hints had fallen on deaf ears, I muttered, 'You'll be lucky,' at the door Harry had let swing behind him. But lucky they were. Indeed, the suggestion that they drive along the coast for the weekend was snapped up eagerly. Minna was thrilled to show them her brand-new baby, and the sainted Elise apparently greeted the two young people as if they were long-lost family. Presumably with no extra barn in hand to offer the happy pair, she had to make do with bestowing her blessing – and going as far as hinting to Minna by the Sunday night that the only thing standing between Tara and the role of perfect godmother at little Pansy's coming christening was the fact that she wasn't yet married to Harry.

'Strange that this Tara even gets to see my baby grand-daughter before I do,' Geoff groused, serving me notice with the unthinking little 'I' and 'my' that, now both his children appeared to be settling nicely after the troubles of the year before, I had gone back to being the invisible woman. It suited me. Invisibility can work two ways and, when you choose to let it, the habit of ignoring a partner's claims may prove profitably catching. Within the last month, Mother had taken a definite turn for the worse. To me she looked the same: grey, curled and silent in her long barred cot. But one by one the nurses who popped in on me as I sat watching let drop sufficient hints to make it clear the end was coming fast. Ed made the noises but he didn't book the flight, even after the final news came.

He did at least apologize. 'I feel a bit bad, Til, leaving all the arrangements to you. But, as you know, it is my busiest time. And, after all, if you look at it sensibly, what's the point?'

'So I'll just get on with it, shall I?'

'If you don't mind.'

And, if I'm honest, I preferred to sort things out alone. But what are you supposed to do with half the things in that last cardboard box? Spectacles still bearing fingerprints from the last time she made the effort to try to read a paper. Greetings cards that survived the last clear-out. The crucifix she never wore but couldn't bring herself to throw away. And photos. Photos of dogs and Christmases, nephews and holidays, babies and gardens. All the detritus of a life that really finished years before. As quickly as I could, I rooted through for any official-looking papers I might need, then slammed the cardboard flaps down on the rest. Instead of setting off for home, I made excuses to Geoff ('Just one or two more things to wrap up here') and drove off the other way. It took a couple of hours, but finally I was back where I had driven in such a rage so many years before. The weather-beaten sign to Folly Leap still hung precariously from its post at the last fork in the road. From the outside, the small hotel looked just the same, but this time I didn't stop. Instead, I took the car as far as I dared along the old dirt track that used to lead to Lartington Tower before the cliff crumbled. The place seemed very different without the comfort of moonlight. The last hundred yards were still fenced off for safety. I didn't even bother to lock the car. The dark was so deep, even the most sharp-eyed thief would not have noticed it, hard up against the starless wall of black above the ocean. Lifting the box off the passenger seat, I rested it on the top of the DANGER! DO NOT VENTURE BEYOND THIS POINT sign as I climbed the gate, then carried it, step by careful step, over the ruts and tussocks of grass, to the cliff edge.

And there I hurled the very last things over. The chain of the crucifix swirled away into darkness. The greetings cards took wing for a moment as the night wind lifted them, then they too were swallowed into black. I heard the tinkling of the spectacles as, tumbling, they caught a few feet down the cliff. Over it all went – mother's vaccination certificates, the last school report card of which she was so proud, even the tiny vase I filled with daisies once when she was sick. Over they went: comb, nail clippers, hairbrush, scissors, leftover shampoo – even the half-empty box of someone else's tissues that happened to be beside her bed on the morning she died. Over and gone, all of it, everything useless and valueless, into the dark, down to the rocks on which waves crashed.

The rest of it I took back home with me. If you're not stupefied with grief, all the procedures after a death seem remarkably simple. The terms of the will were clear – a simple brother and sister two-way split – and, making a fairly informed guess at the final amount after the bills were paid and taxes cleared, I realized I was quite grateful that Geoff had once again hoisted his personal flag over his own family. Indeed, I was pretty well sitting there waiting for the moment he brandished it, ready to pounce.

It wasn't long.

'Is this you up in Aberdeen right through till Friday, Tilly?' Geoffrey stabbed at the line I'd pencilled on the calendar. 'Because I was thinking of phoning Minna again and asking if this week would be any better for me to go down south and meet my grandchild.'

I. Me. My. Gone were the days of resentment. I could be all co-operation now that the grandchild Geoffrey didn't want to share had been matched by the inheritance I didn't want to share either. 'No, no. You go, if it suits Minna this time. Go and enjoy yourself.' I made for the door, then turned as if I'd just remembered something. 'Oh, by the way, I had the most amazing phone call today. I tried to ring you but there were problems in the radio room. It seems that Mother's left all her money to a cats' home.'

Admittedly I'd just come back from three grim weeks off Tripoli. We had crap welders. There had been troubles with the crane. And just as things were coming right again, we had hit shallow gas.

But still. Bloody hell. A cats' home!

Clearly Geoff thought the same. 'A *cats*' home? *All* of it? You must be *joking*, Tilly!' He looked totally baffled. 'Surely your mother didn't even *have* a cat.'

Too late by then to go back and start again with some more credible deception. 'Not at the end, no. But we had cats when Ed and I were growing up, and Mum was always very fond of them.'

'Maybe she was. But that's no reason why they should fart through silk!'

The further his jaw dropped, the madder my whole lie sounded. I set about embroidering as fast as I could. 'Well, as I understand it, the place has other animals as well. Donkeys, I think.' I grew expansive. 'In fact, it's more a rescue centre, really.' Geoff looked so angry I foresaw trouble on another front and added hastily, 'But, after all, since it was Mother's money it was her decision. And this is a will she made well before she went bats.'

He stared at me. 'You don't seem very upset. I can't *believe* it. For seven years you drove down to that godforsaken place to visit her, and now she's left the whole lot to some mangy moggies!' He took a fresh tack. 'What will Ed say, for pity's sake? Surely he'll contest the will?' Geoff gave me the most mistrustful look. 'Tilly, you look so *calm*. Did you already *know* about all this?'

'No,' I said, most sincerely. And it was true that, till the astonishing claim popped out of my mouth, I hadn't given this particular whopper a moment's thought as a way of concealing Mum's money.

Geoff shook his head in wonder. 'I can't *imagine* what your brother will say.'

I could, so I made a point of ringing him as soon as Geoff left the house. Ed roared with laughter. 'Tilly, you are *cruel*. You're *wicked*. You are a *witch*! How could you tell the poor sod something like that?'

I said, a little ruefully, 'It came out all too easily. You promise that you won't let on?'

Ed's silence lasted for a little too long.

I made the promise easier for him to keep. 'After all, I can't think how I'll keep on managing if Geoff ever realizes . . .'

'What do you mean?'

'Well, you know our Geoff. Money dribbles away through his fingers. If I can't keep my half of the inheritance safe, it won't be long before I'm round to your house with the begging bowl.'

Ed took the point. 'All right. I won't say anything. But you're a nasty piece of work, Til. You could at least have told him she'd left it to starving children or limbless ex-servicemen, or something a little more worthy.' He burst out laughing again. 'My God! A cats' home! Mother! Just imagine!'

And certainly I don't know what possessed me. But what had been the result of being too tired to think straight turned out to be a smart move. The thing is, even-stevens makes you happier. Revenge can heal. It makes it easier to be – even to want to be – a much nicer person. After I'd lied so horribly to Geoffrey, I found myself rushing out to buy him a nice suit exactly the same way an errant husband hurries home filled with affection for the wife and laden with flowers. And Geoff's response to what he took to calling 'your mother's brainstorm' brought home to me again in force the unalloyed good nature of his temperament. What was quite obvious was that the man was worrying only on my account, not on his own. The money meant nothing to him. Once I had managed to convince him I wasn't deeply hurt, he let the matter drop at once. There was no nagging me to go to court to lay my mother's wishes aside, no tiresome remarks about the things that I might have chosen to do differently if I had seen this coming. With Geoff, as ever, it was easy come and easy go, and I was pleasantly reminded of why I'd stayed with him so many years. We went to bed a lot. And, almost to thank him for being the obliging man he was, I lashed out on a most luxurious holiday. His brand-new boss at Stationery Supplies offered him unpaid leave to match the days I'd clocked up staying well away from Harry, and off we went. I was delighted by the thought of three weeks free from Geoffrey's forlorn moods each time Minna told him it wasn't quite the best time for him to come down and meet little

Pansy. And Harry's crassly insensitive announcement that he and Tara would soon be moving south as well, to be 'nearer both families', played a large part in making Geoffrey grateful to get away.

It was a brilliant holiday, and once Geoff had been persuaded to lay family disappointments aside, we had the grandest time. The sea I'd come to regard as an ever-present danger raging below became, on that balmy island, a soft pet lapping at my toes. We ate like hungry wolves and slept like bears. And our sheer pleasure in each other's company lasted till we came home. Perhaps the resort itself, so like a Shangri-La, had put Geoff back in the old frame of mind of thinking himself in Happy Valley. His optimism on the flight home was almost painful. 'What's the betting little Pansy's put on a pound or two and is sleeping much better, and I'll be allowed to go down and see her at last?' And as the plane grazed the tarmac: 'I expect Harry's having second thoughts about moving so far away.'

The instant we were in the house he rushed to the answerphone, and even before I'd gathered the last letters off the mat he was running through the messages.

Then he was in the doorway. 'Nothing.'

'What, not from *either* of them?'

'No – unless there's something wrong with the machine.' The sheer unlikelihood of only his son and daughter's messages vanishing into the ether struck him at once. He faced facts. 'Nothing.'

Even I was startled. 'In three whole weeks!'

'We're has-beens,' Geoffrey told me mournfully. 'They have their own lives now, and we don't even rate a simple message about whether Tara and Harry found any flats down south they really liked, or from Minna about Pansy's first tooth or whatever.'

'Not *teeth*,' I said. 'Surely not teeth already.' But what I really wanted to say was, 'No, Geoff. Not "we". Don't try to count me in on these things now, just because you feel lonely.' Seething, I left the room. And mercifully the last two messages were about a problem with the new portable high-pressure wash-down pumps, so I could pretend to be busy till Geoffrey was asleep.

Next day I phoned Sol. 'Any post for me?'

'You're a bad girl, Til,' he scolded. 'And, it seems, a bad girl with quite a large nest-egg.'

'You've shoved it safely into an account, I hope.'

'Already ticking over – though they are insisting you sign some forms.' He coughed politely. 'And, in return for the favour . . . ?'

'Thursday,' I told him. 'Weather permitting, the heiress will be back on shore by noon. I'll drive straight down.'

I'd always loved the way Sol chuckled. 'There's my Bad Tilly. I'll be sitting up in bed, waiting with champagne.'

Finally, halfway through April, the invitation came to meet the baby. Geoff was ecstatic. 'Minna's just rung. They're going to have the christening next month. In the village church. And we're invited.' His face dropped just a little. 'Though Minna did warn me that, what with Elise not having quite enough

bedrooms in the main house for all her guests, she and Josh
have had to offer to put up a couple of nephews.'

'You mean there won't be room for us to stay?'

'It seems not.'

'And I suppose it hasn't occurred to Josh to ask his parents,
who live round the corner.'

'I did try hinting. But Minna said Natalie and Caspar have
been so wonderful with the baby that she doesn't feel she can
ask them to spend any more of their time on other members of
her family.'

'So we're in Bed and Breakfast, are we?' Rather than dwell
on Minna's sheer ungraciousness, I took a fresh tack. 'And will
Tara be godmother, even though she and Harry aren't yet
married?'

Geoff's face lit up again. 'Good news there! It seems that,
what with the wedding date at least being fixed, even Elise
thinks—'

I interrupted him. 'I didn't know.'

'What?'

'That. About the wedding date being fixed.'

'Well, no. Minna's only just told me.'

Easy to look back now and wonder if he wasn't a shade too
glib. And, if I'm honest, I remember thinking it strange even
back then that news of his son's marriage took second place to
the news of the baby's christening. But all I said was, 'Fixed for
when?'

'First week of June, apparently.'

And that's where we came in, of course. 'What, before the

eighth?' I'd said as I stared at him. 'It's the week of the in-spections. You know they're always at the start of June.'

He couldn't say it fast enough. 'I'll ring Harry tomorrow.'

I felt such irritation. 'You can't do that. We haven't even been invited yet.' To stop him trying to fob me off with his benighted optimism about his uncaring children, I spelled it out. 'You can't go telling them to change the dates for some-thing you still only know about by accident.'

The last words clearly stung. 'Scarcely by accident!'

I wasn't going to let him off the hook. 'I don't see what else you'd call it. It's not as if Harry's had the courtesy to ring up and ask, after all. "Oh, by the way, Dad, Tara and I are thinking of getting married. Would this date be all right for you and Tilly?"'

'So are you saying I should just let them carry on with the arrangements as they are now?'

'I think that's best. After all, *you* can still go.' I turned sarcastic. 'And it won't be the first time I'll have missed a family occasion.'

Instantly, he made for the phone. 'Well, I am going to ring them.'

'No!'

'Now you're just being silly.'

What is it about men, that they're so quick to disparage a woman's emotions? 'Don't call my feelings "being silly", please. Your son's wedding matters to you, but my pride matters to me and I don't want you phoning on my account. If it's their choice not to check dates with me, it's equally my choice not to have you ring them.'

Unable to argue the point, Geoffrey changed tack. 'Look, I expect they just didn't think about it.'

I acted as incredulous as I felt. 'How would they not think about it? Harry knows my job. He knows that once a year I go off on inspections and that the schedule is set in stone. If he was bothered, he'd have phoned to check.'

He tried another blind alley. 'Surely I could just mention it . . .'

But I'd had enough. 'Oh, for Christ's sake, Geoff! Haven't you learned yet that, in a family like this, there's no such thing as "simply mentioning" something?'

He didn't answer, so I just slammed out. I skipped the christening. After all, she wasn't my grandchild, and Cornwall's a long way away. I can't remember what excuse I gave. I do know where I was, because Sol and I did take the trouble to raise a glass of bubbly to the child, and wish her well. 'What family occasion are you missing next?' Sol asked me gallantly as we fell apart. 'May I put it down now in my diary?' 'Certainly,' I answered. 'It will be the third of June. Harry and Tara's wedding. But, tragically, I'll be in the North Sea, prowling round looking for unauthorized modifications and other safety lapses.'

'Ah. The famous inspections.'

But, as I said, what with the blow-out at Troendseim, the inspections were all delayed and I ended up at the wedding. And wasn't I glad about that! I look back now and realize that, without that bright morning in Sussex, I might have carried on for years more living in half-light. Why, I might still be there, watching him blind himself to the truth about his self-centred children, and pretending to share his life in cloud cuckoo land.

The day started well enough. Tara's widowed mother greeted us warmly. She seemed an unassuming soul, with bandages on her legs, and was disposed to think me wonderful from the start because, seeing the caterer anxiously struggling with his hot-water urn, I'd strolled across to diagnose the problem. 'How clever of you!' she enthused when I came back, as if I'd single-handedly designed a desalination plant, not simply shifted an air lock. 'I'm lost in admiration. Harry, dear, did you see what your mother just—'

She stopped, aghast at herself. 'I'm sorry. I mean, your *step*m—'

She broke off again, clearly the sort of woman who thinks that calling someone a stepmother is much the same as calling her a witch. 'Tilly!' she said at last, her voice strangled with relief. 'Harry, did you see what *Tilly* here has managed?' And you could see from the look on her face as she hobbled away to welcome the next arrivals that, in her own mind, working out what it was polite to call me had been just as inventive and admirable as fixing her tea urn.

Geoff led me off the other way, over the daisied lawn. Then suddenly he gripped my arm. 'There they are! There!' he cried, quite as excitedly as if we'd been looking for elephants. 'I thought they'd arrive a whole lot later, coming all the way from Torbury Bay – and with a baby.'

'Maybe they came yesterday.'

'They can't have. Minna thought I'd be spending yesterday

evening all alone in that place down the road. If they'd been staying anywhere locally, I'm sure she would have let me know.'

I didn't argue. Nobody sits in a car for that length of drive without creasing their clothing. But Geoff was clearly set fair to enjoy the day, floating above brute truth. It's just that I couldn't face being part of his idiot enthusiasm. 'You say hello to them all,' I whispered, 'while I slip off to the loo. Back in a minute.'

I dawdled in the lavatory behind the conservatory, putting on more and more lipstick until I heard a fierce rustling outside. The handle rattled. I unlocked the door. There stood a woman in a hat with flowers dancing on wires. 'Thank God!' she said. 'I'm *bursting*.' So off I went to find the others again, hoping that by now everyone would be so sick of introductions that they would let me slide in unannounced.

Not a chance. 'So *this* is the famous Tilly!' the man I took to be Minna's new father-in-law trumpeted. Instantly his wife tried to deflect him. 'Don't, Caspar! You'll make poor Tilly think that we've been talking about her behind her back.'

Up till she said it, the notion had never even occurred to me. (And, in my whole life, I don't believe that anyone has ever had the nerve to call me 'poor Tilly'.) I raised an eyebrow at Minna, but she just clung to Josh's arm and nodded briefly as if, far from being someone who'd read her bedtime stories, bathed her cuts and tested her on French vocabulary, I was some neighbour she had once or twice passed on the street.

Meanwhile, the ghastly Natalie turned back to me. 'You

missed little Pansy's christening!' she said, gripping the handle
of her granddaughter's pram and staring at me as if she and her
family had travelled across five counties to this wedding
simply for some explanation. Since I could scarcely say the
prospect of being ignored by Minna and patronized by her new
family had failed to appeal enough for me to accept their
remarkably offhand invitation, I just remarked on how much
Geoffrey had enjoyed the day. (And it was true he'd come home
from the visit happy enough. Pansy had favoured him with
smile after smile, so he had nice photos; and the sainted Elise
had apparently even been kind enough to ask some hapless
nephew to show Geoff round Minna and Josh's 'barn' while
everyone else was busy with friends who'd strolled in from the
village.)

Minna's new mother-in-law now smiled forgivingly. 'Well,
at least you get to meet Pansy today.'

A voice behind me, drawling with graciousness, asked, '*Who*
gets to meet Pansy?' Everyone jumped to attention. 'Elise!'
cried Natalie, seemingly thrilled to see her mother again after
a gap of what can only have been a few minutes. 'It's Tilly,
Minna's stepmother, come to say hello at last.'

Since it was stalking off or turning round, I felt obliged to
turn. I let the imperious old trout who'd just crept up on us
inspect me up and down, pricing my wardrobe and appraising
my vivid hair. I ignored her unpleasant suggestion that I'd preferred to spend my time with 'all those men in Aberdeen'
rather than come to the christening, and even tried to continue
to look pleasant while the ghastly old bag proffered her airily

insincere assurance that she and her daughter and son-in-law 'might perhaps think of inviting you and your . . .' The long, long silence was followed by a discreet cough of disapproval but no actual *word*. '. . . to come to visit us again one day.'

Then, having had enough of Minna's frightful new family, I made my escape.

It isn't easy to lurk at a wedding as firmly organized as Tara and Harry's. At some invisible signal, everyone was flushed away from the tea and coffee urns and herded in line along the wide flat freshly mown grass verge towards the village church. Here we were shepherded into pews according to some printed plan. 'I'm surprised Tara hasn't stuck colour-coded stickers on all her guests,' I whispered to Geoffrey. The service started dead on time, as I had known it would. The choir sang for their lives, with fussy descants warbling up and away into the rafters. The only bright spot was the moment I glanced at the words on my printed hymn sheet and noticed that, by a tiny misprint even the assiduous Tara had overlooked, we were about to sing our praises not to God but to Gold.

Geoff faked a coughing fit to cover my snigger and kept a warning hand on my arm till, in strict sequence, we were ushered out again and back along the road to the marquee. The lady with the hat with the flowers on wires had clearly taken our meeting in the lavatory to be the start of a friendship. 'See?' she said proudly, pointing along the tables we happened to be approaching at the same time. 'A buffet – and no queue! How often have you seen that?' She tugged each of her high heels in turn out of the turf as the flowers danced over her head. 'That's clever Tara for you.' She sighed expansively. 'Not that it makes any difference to me. I shan't be filling a plate. In the summer, I am virtually a *fruitbat*!'

Geoffrey came up behind us. 'May I help you two lovely ladies to your tables?'

My new companion drifted away as mysteriously as she'd arrived. I laid a hand on Geoffrey's arm. 'When can we go?' He looked so shocked, I added hastily, 'What I mean is, should I stop drinking now? How long till we'll be driving home?'

Geoffrey's relief was obvious. 'No, no. Don't worry about that. Let's find our places, shall we?'

'Places?'

But, yes. It seemed that Tara's drive towards efficiency meant, even at a buffet, a place for everyone and everyone in his place. On account of a rather intriguing spatial anomaly created by putting an oblong table behind a kidney-shaped flower bed next to a semicircular dip dividing the lawn from the orchard, I ended up one seat along from Geoffrey but nowhere near him. Instead, I found myself sitting between Tara's deaf great-uncle and some pompous old fart who talked only of investments. Across the table, a mother and daughter had surreptitiously swapped place cards around so they could whisper continually through the meal, ignoring the young man they'd displaced. He clearly didn't care. In any event, so far as I could tell the switch was to his benefit. As long as he could keep up the pretence I wasn't sitting opposite with no one to talk to, he could – and did – give all his attention to shovelling food into his mouth.

'Are you a friend of Tara's?' I leaned across to ask him after he came back with thirds.

'God, no!' he said. 'I'm her brother,' and set about wolfing yet again, as if he were fresh from a cage. In the end I gave up and went back to the lavatory. When I was rattled out a second time, the queue of bursting ladies stretched way down the hall. I took my time strolling back, but when I looked in, waiters were clearing everything except glasses and coffee cups. Clearly, the speeches were about to start. I couldn't face it. Hoping that Geoffrey hadn't spotted my brief reappearance between the marquee's pinned-back flaps, I once again turned round and vanished.

Geoff found me sitting on the stone ledge of the goldfish pond, teasing the fish. 'Tilly? I thought we'd lost you. Are you feeling left out?'

'No,' I said. 'I was just on my way back when I noticed these and stopped for a moment.' I gave him a close look. 'Why? Are you?'

'What?'

'Feeling left out.'

'No, not at all,' he said, for all the world as if I hadn't seen the way Elise and Natalie had shifted his chair to the very end of the table so they could fit the pram between the two of them and keep up a steady conversation over its canopy, ignoring Geoff entirely. But what was the point of saying anything? The man must be back in Noddyland if he couldn't see his daughter had willingly surrendered herself body and soul to Josh's family. And who could blame her? After a diet of parental separation, illness and death, they offered a fresh start. The only pity was that their strength was founded on the twin pillars of Elise's steel will and Natalie's complacency. Already it was clear that offering hospitality to Minna's relations was not what they had in mind at all; and only someone as boyishly optimistic as Geoff could fail to see that, so coolly sidelined over a single formal lunch, he'd be wasting his time hoping warmer invitations might drop on his doormat.

But clearly the question I'd turned back on him had set him thinking. 'Well, a little left out, perhaps.' He patted his pocket. 'I mean, it was a very *short* speech. And I would so much have liked to welcome Tara into the family.'

Ashamed that I'd clean forgotten, I tried to be sympathetic. 'Just a mistake, I expect. It probably slipped Harry's mind to mention to anyone that you wanted to say a few words.'

As ever, he was quick off the mark in defence of his off-spring. 'No, no. The problem was Tara.' He saw my questioning look. 'It seems she wasn't sure that it was suitable.'

'Suitable?'

'You know.' He scraped a polished shoe sideways along the stone ledge. 'What with the way we are.'

I was mystified. 'What way?'

'Not *married* properly, Til. You know that Tara takes her religious beliefs extremely seriously.' He dropped his voice. 'In fact, I rather think that might be one of the reasons Harry was so keen to get the knot safely tied even before he's finished college.'

'To get a bit of nooky?'

Geoffrey ignored this. 'And for much the same reasons — caring so much about these things, I mean — it seems that Tara didn't think it was quite right to have someone who was living in sin make a speech at her wedding.'

I snorted with amusement. ' "Living in sin"? Is that how she put it? Snotty litttle cow!' I was laughing so hard I nearly fell into the fishpond. Geoff had to put out a hand to steady me. When I got a grip of myself, I asked him, still amused: 'And Harry put up with all this?'

'Harry's in love. And it is Tara's day, of course.'

But give some people the wedding day and they'll take the next day and the next, and every single day after that. And there's no fighting a Christian. If Geoff and I were 'living in sin' now, we'd probably be 'the Devil and all his works' by the time any children came. After all, anyone who can rid a lunch buffet of queues can get rid of relations they don't want. Already I could hear the sound of doors being slammed and bolted.

I slid off the ledge and brushed the stone grit from the back of my skirt. Holding my hand out, I said, 'Come on, Geoff. Let's go back and face the enemy.' He saw me to my seat, then, finding that in his short absence his own had already been folded to make more space for the pram, went off to find another place.

Aching with boredom, I sat through the last of the speeches,

tirelessly folding and refolding discarded paper nests from all
the *petits fours* Tara's brother was still industriously scoffing. I
couldn't help it. I was sunk in gloom. With son and daughter
gone, who did that leave for Geoffrey? Me. The feeling of being
trapped swept over me so strongly, I might have been behind
steel bars. Certainly I was the only guest at the table to ignore
hints to leave. I let the waiters bustle their way towards me,
sweeping up silverware and bundling up tablecloths. Filled
with resentful thoughts, I hatched a childish plan to take
revenge on the day by stealing the sugar spoon in front of me.
Shaped like a flat-bottomed ladle, it was the mirror image of
one my grandmother always promised to leave me – my
favourite thing in her whole house. I must have spent hours at
her kitchen table sprinkling caster sugar through its pattern of
tiny holes, over and over, as Ed and I waited for our mother to
get back from her myriad jaunts and excursions. It vanished in
the frenzied grab-fest after my grandmother's death, and at the
time I didn't think much of it. But as I sat there, watching the
waiters clear a score of spoons just like it off the other tables, I
suddenly wanted this one badly enough to inch my handbag
closer to the legs of my chair, take out a tissue and pretend to
sneeze.

I had the spoon safely under the tissue when a shadow fell at
my side, startling me horribly.

'Hi, Tilly!' Harry gave me an affectionate hug. 'I'm so glad
it all worked out all right.'

I could have responded sourly, 'Yes – but thanks only to the
worst blow-out in the Company's history.' But I couldn't see

the point. If Harry wanted to fall into his father's habit of thinking everything would come out tickety-boo without his efforts, that was up to him. He was a married man now. Tara's problem, not mine. It was easier to be pleasant. 'It's been a *lovely* wedding,' I assured him, taking the opportunity to slide the spoon and tissue off the table onto my lap, and keeping my hands clasped demurely on top of them.

Harry pulled out a chair and sank down beside me. 'No, no,' he said. 'I meant with the inspections – first week of June, and all that. I was quite worried.'

I was so taken up with wondering how to move the spoon into my bag, I barely heard him. 'Oh, well. As you say, it all worked out.'

'Yes. Dad said he'd talk to you about it, and since it was a wedding, you'd probably be allowed to switch things round this once.'

I might have been distracted, but this still sank in. 'Did he?'

'Yes. And he was right!' Harry grinned. 'Thank God! Because the whole business of arranging dates was a nightmare, Tilly. Tara was quite fixated on the idea of June because of her dad, of course.'

'Because of her dad?'

'Yes. Saying before he died that, right from the day she was born, he'd had this vision of giving her away at her wedding on a lovely June day. And that he wanted her to promise that, even though he now knew he wouldn't be there to do it himself—' He broke off. 'Well, you heard her Uncle Jim's speech.'

I could scarcely admit I hadn't. So I just smiled and nodded sympathetically as I slid the tissue and spoon off my lap into my handbag. Pressing the bundle down, my fingers caught on a small folded square of paper and for a moment I couldn't think what it might be, or why I'd tucked it in there.

But Harry was off again. 'So!' He was spreading his hands triumphantly. 'You were the hero of the hour, Til! Because either we would have had to wait another whole year, or Tara's mum would have had to wave goodbye to the deposit she'd just put down on her holiday. Dad said he'd talk to you, and look! You're here as promised.'

High as a kite with happiness, he gave me another hug. My brain was spinning. What had the boy just said? 'We would have had to wait another whole year'? What, with the date of the wedding already spread around? And what was all that about Tara's mother changing her holiday plans? Why should that even have fetched up as an issue, if the fact that I was committed to the inspections hadn't been part of the discussion right from the start?

Maybe it was. The longer I thought about it, the more possible it seemed. Take Harry's blithe 'Dad said, since it was a wedding, you'd probably be allowed to switch things round.' I'd taken Harry merely to be repeating some typically emollient Geoffism after the date had been fixed, so he would not have to confront his son with hurt at the bridal couple's sheer insensitivity. But could it have been said a good deal earlier?

Before the plans were fully made?

I stared in the dark mouth of the bag clutched on my knee.

My powder compact, lipstick, cheque card, tissues, car keys, comb. And there, tucked in amongst them, the little folded note.

Could it be possible? Was there truly hope?

'So where is Gloria going on this holiday?' I asked, to buy more time to work things out.

'One of those frondy islands in the Seychelles, I think.'

'Lovely! Next week?'

'Tomorrow.' The mention of time brought Harry back to the present. He rose from the table. 'Married man now, eh? Got to follow orders. Better keep mingling.'

'Yes. That's the ticket, Harry.'

As soon as he'd gone, I drew the note out of the handbag, fresh and clear as the day I had forced Geoff to write it. *No lies, no leaving information out, no sneaky little deceptions of any sort. That is the deal.* And, underneath, the old familiar signature written a little unsteadily from the sheer shock of the demand. Don't get your hopes up, I told myself. Don't think too far ahead. Harry's account of things might have been garbled with champagne and the excitement of the prospect of his first night with his virgin bride. Perhaps he has the story all mixed up.

My knees were shaking as I left the marquee and worked my way round the garden (carefully avoiding Geoffrey) in search of the one person who might, by a word let drop, send me home singing.

At last I found her.

'Gloria!' (Step carefully, Tilly.) 'A wonderful wedding! Brilliantly organized and everything perfect. I was just thinking you must be absolutely ready for a break after all the upheaval. And now your brand-new son-in-law tells me you're off to the Seychelles.'

She launched into the details of her holiday. I didn't have to prompt. Out it all came – how she decided where to go, what made her choose that travel company, and the fright when she thought she would lose her deposit.

'So *frustrating*,' I murmured sympathetically. 'If you leave cancelling till too late, you can be charged almost the full cost of the holiday.'

She looked quite shocked. 'Really? My golly! I was lucky, then. I only stood to lose a couple of hundred pounds.' Discreetly, she dropped her voice. 'But after all, this trip's not going to be at all cheap, so even that would have been irritating.'

In my mind's eye I had the sharpest image of Geoffrey, way back in April, hanging up the phone starry-eyed at the news of the christening. I heard our voices as clearly as if the little exchange had taken place yesterday: 'What with the wedding date at least being fixed . . .' 'I didn't know.' 'Well, no. Minna's only just told me.'

I took the deepest breath. 'So,' I asked Gloria innocently, 'what notice did you manage to give? A full month?'

She stared as if she thought I might be tipsy. '*Three* months, Tilly.' Scrabbling in her handbag, she pulled out the packet she'd been hiding from Tara all day, and tapped out a cigarette. 'To the day, in fact. I remember distinctly because the woman in the travel office said she'd only been able to save me from losing a single penny because her computer had been down the

day before.' She glanced round nervously to check her daughter
wasn't watching her, then lit her cigarette and took a deep
drag. 'So wasn't I lucky?' Like some sophisticated dragon, she
let the smoke slide out of one side of her mouth. 'Tilly?'

I don't know what she thought she was seeing on my face.
Exhilaration? Relief? Pure blinding ecstasy? Perhaps she took
me for the sort of soppy soul prepared to be thrilled by
somebody else's good fortune. In any case, she grasped my arm
and told me warmly, 'Though of course, Tilly, by rights it's you
I have to thank for offering to switch your work dates around
so very promptly.' She gave a throaty giggle. 'Really I ought to
buy you a drink, but—'

I don't know how she would have finished up. Perhaps:
'— but it's a free bar.' Or even, '— but it looks to me as if you
might have had a few already.' But I had interrupted. 'I must
say, Gloria, if you really do feel that you owe me a favour, I
wouldn't say no to one of your cigarettes.'

She beamed. 'Another smoker? Bliss!' She peered round,
clearly still on the look-out for her stern daughter, then offered
furtively, 'Come round the back of the marquee and we can sin
together.'

We picked our way in our high heels around the guy ropes.
I clutched my handbag safely to my side, all too aware of its
precious paper cargo. However you stretch it, halfway through
April to the first week in June is not three months. And there,
hidden safe inside, lay my reprieve, fresh as the day I dictated
it: *No lies, no leaving information out, no sneaky little deceptions of
any sort. That is the deal.*

199

My open sesame. My brand-new passport out.

I took the cigarette that Gloria offered me. As I inexpertly puffed great clouds around us, then fell into splutters, the dizzying feeling of freedom grew and the coughs turned to laughter. Suddenly I found myself confessing to my hostess with perfect honesty, 'You see, the problem is that I don't smoke really, Gloria. Never – well, hardly ever. Only if, like today, it is a very, *very* special occasion.'

12

THAT IS WEAK PEOPLE FOR YOU. THEIR ONLY STRENGTH LIES IN their little secrets. The only power that they have comes from keeping things from others. And, *bingo*! That was it. Geoffrey had hanged himself on the old, old habit. The only question was, why had he been so stupid as to try and grub up a tiny bit of goodwill from a woman he hadn't even met yet, at such risk to his life with me? I can only assume he was confident I wouldn't find out – or, if I did, that he'd be able to ride out the storm. It was that same incorrigible complacency that causes all too many husbands to lose their wives – that lasting and impregnable assumption that, just because they themselves are too smug and idle either to change themselves or anything around them, the woman they live with will not rouse herself to change anything either. Geoff knew as well as I did that our life together was built on a fault line. Right from the start we'd felt the tremors and quakes. What Geoff had chosen to forget is that it's both halves of a couple, and not just one, who are free to decide that some companionable old rift has become an unbridgeable chasm. He thought I'd stay because to stay was easy, and idleness ran through him like letters stamped through seaside rock. It stopped him ever facing facts that might have stirred his stumps. But one of the facts that he'd refused to face was that my life with him had always had one thing in common with that marriage to Bill which ended with such ease: it wasn't the time we spent together that kept it going, but the time we spent apart. We had no joint ambitions and no common plan. We didn't even share passions. In fact, I felt like someone living in a pleasant hotel. I was well fed, the rooms were comfortable, and, day to day, everything ran on oiled wheels. But, at heart, none of it was anything to do with me. That was the way he had preferred to keep things, and that's the way they'd grown.

But in the end everyone gets to choose. And you can settle for emotional fog blurring the edges of failure. Or you can get out.

Interesting that they all tried stopping me. 'He probably thought he was just being nice.' Donald tried to defend him.

'*Nice?* Telling some stranger in Sussex I'll be able to make a date I won't, just to save her the inconvenience of shifting her holiday?'

'You know how these things happen. You want to be helpful and it just sort of slips out because it would be so convenient if it were true.'

Ed said the same. 'Oh, Tilly. Why make such a meal of it?

The poor clown probably intended to 'fess up from the moment he said it, then simply didn't dare.'

Next time we slept together, I asked Sol, 'Why wouldn't he have *said*?'

Sol pushed the flaming curtain of my hair away to stare at me somewhat incredulously, but all he said (and rather mildly) was, 'Tilly, you are a rather frightening person when you get angry.'

So there you are. Three men. And all agreed on it. All sticking up for one another, as usual. I have to admit it enraged me. All week I stamped round the rig, staring at all those signs I'd copied out to intrigue Harry all those years ago. NO SMOKING, NO EATING, NO DRINKING. NO ENTRY BEYOND THIS POINT WITHOUT A SAFETY HARNESS. YOU BREAK THIS RULE, WE FLY YOU OUT. And that does happen. Only the week before, we'd lost a good motor man simply because he wouldn't follow the company rules about pushing wheeled gear along catwalks. Oh, yes! Men can be quick enough to act if the issue is one, like an all too likely compensation claim, that might affect company profits. Or to squawk if it personally affects *them*. Try cheating Sol on a deal, and I can't see you coming out unscathed. I wouldn't mess with my brother about things that matter to him. And as for Donald – even mild-mannered Donald – try telling lies to him about whether or not you'll make it up to Aberdeen in time for the next relay out. You'll soon see your cards in your hand. But point out some personal betrayal that matters to you, and they'll be practically queuing up to urge you to let it slide. 'Come off it,

Tilly. He was trying to be nice' (or 'keep the peace'; or 'stop you getting upset'; or any one of a million excuses for not having the guts to be straight). They just can't see decisions have to rest on something over and above just being 'nice'. Once you start off down that street, we could all go round making other people's lives a misery, all the while telling ourselves we're acting from the best of motives. It would turn out as easy to call Geoff a fine upstanding man for trying to save Gloria a pittance as label him craven for telling lies to me, presumably in order to keep a little bit of an edge on his own family – the only thing he had and I didn't. The only thing that was still offering him a tiny bit of self-esteem.

But it's not for each of us to decide for ourselves which things in life are going to be important. We have to get a grip on our subconscious minds, the feelings we hide, not just from others but from ourselves as well. We have to live so others know where they stand. That's why, beneath the surface crap of things like good manners and a reasonable amount of willing helpfulness, lie other, tougher things. Because they're more important, they're even given a different name. We call them *virtues*.

And one of the virtues is honesty. But none of them could see it. They simply couldn't see it. 'You've made me tell a good few whoppers on your behalf,' Donald kept reminding me.

'Hark at the pot moralizing about the kettle,' scoffed Ed. 'Have you forgotten how you lied to Geoff about where Mother's money went? *And* bullied me into supporting you.'

'You are deceitful too,' said Sol. 'I expect you're being deceitful now, simply to be in bed with me.'

I closed my ears to all of them. I refused to listen.

Easy enough to put the question to me now. 'Tilly, why didn't you just walk away?'

You try it. There's a staying quality about weak people no one can match. It is a tyranny. Live with a man while, one by one, he loses his savings and his property, his income and children, and I defy you at the end to have the guts to say to him, 'And now I'm leaving too.' I think I had no choice. You can ask: 'Why didn't you solve the problem by selling up and splitting everything two ways?' I think the answer's clear: why on earth *should* I? I'm not the one who dribbled my assets away, one after another, in the face of all warnings. If you spend years indulging yourself in 'thinking everything will work out right', you can't expect everyone round you to compensate you if things go sour. Fools suffer. That is the way of the world. I might have had a bit more sympathy if Geoff had been an idiot by birth – someone too stupid to understand a contract, or grasp the hidden costs of a loan. But sail through life sunny and carefree, deliberately ignoring the possibility that things might go awry, and you should pay the price.

Besides, it was entirely his choice to try to come after me. (Admittedly I knew he would. But is a woman to be held to blame if a man's made it plain he is unlikely to make the slightest effort to manage without her? If he gets needier and needier over the years, is she supposed to choose only those paths that take into account the fact that, in his determination to be a leech, he might well follow?) All very well for you to say now, so accusingly, 'Tilly, you *must* have known exactly what would happen.' I can still answer fearlessly: 'It's a free country, isn't it? That was up to him.' In any case, the way I looked at it, he'd wasted years of my life. When I met Geoffrey, I was only in my twenties, flame-haired and made for passions that would follow fast on one another's heels. Now I was forty-three, with streaks of grey I couldn't even be bothered to hide, and such a habit of settling for whatever came next that I felt I'd let the life I should have lived slip through my fingers. It seemed to me he'd taken my best years. And, if I'm honest, I was angrier – oh, far, far angrier – than simply wanting to leave.

I wanted to make Geoffrey pay. And pay with interest.

Fascinating, the way the problem of Geoffrey could best be solved by mirroring his habits. Up until then, I'd lied only about the big things: exactly where I was, and who I was sleeping with. That was as easy as blinking compared with keeping petty day-to-day secrets under a shared roof. Having to keep that up really sharpens the wits and stretches the memory. There was a lot to think about and a lot to get done. And all the while, I kept up the steady drip, drip, drip, of pretending that nothing had changed. I fussed about the new rotas. I grumbled endlessly about the one-day safety reviews. I moaned about last-minute crew changes. Nobody listening would ever have thought for a moment I might have been paying sufficient attention over the weeks to work out that the one day Geoff would definitely be away was Harry's graduation.

'Such a pity that each of them is only allowed two guests,' he said for the twentieth time as he polished his shoes again. I could have said that, as the one who'd sat with Harry through a thousand homework sessions, bribing him with cake, I had more claim than Tara to the second ticket. But I sat tight. Nor did I bother to remind him that all those concerts at the primary school, those plays in secondary, and those perennial parent–teacher discussions had had no limits on the numbers at all, and no one had ever expressed the slightest regret about not inviting me to those. I only nodded at the clock. 'Hadn't you better get going? It's a long drive.' To speed him on his way, I added one more lie direct to his face. 'Tara said she and Harry would be there by noon.'

'Really? As early as that?' He reached for his jacket. 'Right. I'm off.'

'What time will you be home?' I asked, as if I actually cared.

He shrugged. 'The ceremony starts at three. How long do these things last?' He made a guess. 'Sixish? Unless the three of us go for a cup of tea after, in which case I suppose it might be seven. Or even a little later.'

'Take all the time you want.' Maybe I even pulled my dressing gown closer around me and yawned, as if to make it clear that today the pressure of time meant nothing. The moment he was out of the house, I threw on my clothes and started dragging the cardboard boxes out from where I'd been storing them flat, hidden away in the garage, sandwiched between the

ladders along the back wall and the huge metal safety sign I'd
smuggled out of the company's on-shore store and into the
back of my car, draped with tarpaulin. I didn't hang about. I
went round the house like a tornado, hurling every last thing
that belonged to either Geoffrey or his children into the boxes.

Less than an hour later, the first of the vans I'd ordered drew
up outside, but I was ready. Checking my way along the pegs
in the hall for any last jackets or scarves I'd overlooked that
belonged to the Andersons, I said to the driver, 'You're sure
you've completely understood? Pack all these boxes in the van.
Lock them up safely, and you're free to do what you want so
long as you're back here by five. And when the owner of this
stuff finally shows up, tell him the deal.'

He reeled it off, parrot-fashion. 'Van fully prepaid for three
days, including the cost of delivery to the address of his choice.'
He added off his own bat, 'Even if it's Cornwall?'

'It might very well be Cornwall,' I warned.

'Or John O'Groats?'

'Less likely,' I admitted, and went back into the house to get
on with the next load of packing.

The second, larger, van arrived an hour later.

'Everything?'

'Everything except carpets and curtains, the ladders in the
garage, the washer, drier . . .' I read them off the list, then
handed it over as an aide-memoire. As we walked through the
house, I glanced across at the old rocking horse I'd bought for
the children. By rights I really should have taken it, if only to
remind me of how hard I was trying, at the start, to welcome

this family under my roof and to become a living part of it. But in the end I decided it would probably only go on reminding me strongly of Bill. 'And that can stay. But everything else is going, and it must all be out by four o'clock.'

'No problem.'

And there wasn't, even with the locksmith getting under everyone's feet as he changed all the door locks. I'd learned the knack over the weeks of sorting things in piles then simply draping one large garment over them to make them look more casual: less a house on the move than something I was sorting out and putting somewhere else.

The removal men swarmed everywhere. 'And the food in these cupboards?'

'That's all to be cleared out. There's someone moving in at five o'clock.'

The one in charge raised an eyebrow. 'Today? Cutting it a bit fine, aren't we?'

'Not if you keep it up at this rate.'

And they did. As fast as they cleared each cupboard, I was there with my cloth, sweeping stray lentils and bits of dried-up pasta out onto the counters below or onto the floor, then wiping and mopping. I don't believe I've ever worked so hard in my whole life or been so glad to hear the words: 'That's it, I reckon.'

The boss and I walked through the house together and checked the garage. 'Pretty good,' I said.

'So we'll be off.' He glanced down at his paperwork to check one last time. 'And it's indefinite storage for the whole lot.' I watched his eyes fall on the four huge black bags I'd filled with perfectly good tins and cereals, sauces and pastas and herbs, and the piles of ready meals from the freezer. 'Want us to do you a favour and drop all this stuff at the dump?' he asked me hopefully.

'Yes, please,' I said, peeling out notes to lay on their outstretched paws. And then, because I have a special responsibility for safety at work, I couldn't help blowing his dignified little deception by saying sternly to all of them, 'Now, remember you must never re-freeze meat or fish. So use those up today or tomorrow, or not at all.'

'Yes, ma'am,' they chorused with that obedient eyes-down look men use when they have other plans. I couldn't bring myself to care. Let the whole pack of them poison themselves, their wives and their children. I simply waved them off down the street, then went back to pick up both new sets of shiny keys. I locked the doors behind me, sat on the step and waited. None of my neighbours was around. No one was watching. No one walked past to say goodbye. It is a dreary area, actually, and I'm not sorry to be done with it.

I didn't have to sit long. Shortly before five, a huge removal van from Newcastle pulled round the corner. I went over to greet it. 'Here are the keys.'

The driver reached down to take them from me. 'Is it your house?'

'No,' I said, presuming that my solicitor had done her job, and by now this was true. 'I'm just a neighbour. I don't know anything at all except that these are the keys.'

The driver transferred his worried look from me to the house. 'Oh, well,' he said. 'The new people aren't far behind. I suppose till they get here we can just use our common sense and guess where they'll want things to go.'

He looked as if it was by no means the first time he'd faced this problem. And, after all, how far wrong can you go, arranging furniture in a small semi-detached house on a small boring street?

I won't say where I went. Some day I might want to go back again, and not be found. Ever. But it was a quiet week. I needed time to think. Sometimes I walked along the coastal paths. It seemed to me the waves were speaking and the moon sent messages. I don't mean I went bats. I mean that all that dark and peace and moonlight seemed to be gathering together to make the decision I made one of significance. I heard it in the rhythm of the waves. Just *do* it, they seemed to be saying as they crashed on the rocks. Just *do* it. *Do* it. All of the reasons not to are puny and unconvincing. Almost absurd.

But it took thought and care. I had to get things right. Finally I made one phone call from outside the pub in this village in the middle of nowhere.

'Tilly! For Christ's sake! Your bloody man's been mooning around outside the gates all week. Security are sick of him. And where the hell are you? You were supposed to be here early this morning, remember?'

'I'm not coming back, Donald.'

'Not coming back?'

'Yup. Finished with the whole boiling.' I carried on into the incredulous silence. 'I'm going to start a brand-new life somewhere abroad,' I lied. 'I'm sorry not to have warned you earlier. It's just that I knew Geoff would be there to look for me this morning. And this way I get a bit of a head start.'

He wasn't pleased. 'So where the fuck are *you*?'

'Gatwick.'

There was a moment's pause in which birds sang in branches above my head and, as if to make my perfidy even more obvious, a duck quacked loudly.

'It doesn't *sound* like Gatwick.'

I gazed across the street to the village green. On a pretty roofed noticeboard there was an exhortation to the local citizenry to come to the meeting about the plan to clean out the old pond. 'That's because I'm in the airport's new Meditation Centre. They run a tape of soothing country sounds.'

Someone walked past me, saying, 'Admiring the ducks on our filthy old pond?'

'And a rather fine mural of wild birds,' I added.

I could tell Donald didn't believe a word of it. I waited while he drew in breath and had a little think. Then he changed tack. 'Look, sweetheart, I do see that having a bit of a stalker must be rather tiresome, even if it is your old man.'

'He's not my old man, Donald. Geoff and I have never married.'

'Keep your hair on, Til. What about getting that other bloke of yours – what's-his-name?'

'Sol.'

'Yes. Can't you make *him* talk to Geoff? Explain what's what, and all that. Get him to tell Geoff his time's up, and he's to hand over his side of the bed with a little more grace.'

Amazing, isn't it? They can't imagine a woman might be set fair to get on with her life without a single one of them grasping her ankles. I didn't bother to argue. After all, the more daft theories in the air when someone vanishes, the more successfully you cloud your exit. 'It's not that, Donald. It's a whole lot bigger than that.'

'What is it, then? *What?*'

'I'm taking a new direction,' I told him. (Choose to be anything. Fly!) Flippantly, I added, 'Maybe I'll go into wind farms. I reckon wind farms are the future. They must be crying out for people like me.'

'Oh, fuck off, Tilly!' he snapped. When he next spoke, he sounded miserable, as if he were the only one of the three who truly loved me. 'Tilly, I'm going to do my level best to hold your job open for you. But if you don't show up, it's out of my hands and you know it. So you had better get your act together pretty quickly.'

I could have told him, 'Don't bother, Donald,' but the line had gone dead.

Then it was back to work, studying the tide tables and the phases of the moon, and when they'd interlink. Meanwhile, I kept track of Geoffrey, secure in the knowledge he couldn't keep track of me without Sol's connivance.

'Twelve, thirteen – fourteen bits of forwarded mail, Til.

Most of it's circulars and other crap. And Donald has sent down seven more letters from Geoffrey.'

'Is he still down in Torbury Bay?'

'No, no. It seems he's worn out his welcome there.'

'Is that what he says?'

'Not exactly.' I heard Sol rustling sheets of letter paper. ' "Please, please write, Til," ' he read out in an only slightly mocking imitation of how he thought Geoffrey might sound. ' "But not to here, because it seems Elise has guests arriving unexpectedly from South Africa. Very old friends. She says she's sorry but she needs the bed. And Tara and Harry say that though it was lovely having me before, now Tara has to get back to her course work, and it's a thing about her, apparently, that she can't concentrate if there is anyone staying in the house." '

'Well-diagnosed. Worn out his welcome there.'

Sol kept on reading through the next disaster. ' "So since Vanguard Direct have as good as warned me they'll have to let me go if I'm not back by Monday—" '

'Vanguard Direct? I thought Geoff worked for Stationery Supplies?'

'He did. Till he was fired for taking too much time off.'

'I didn't know that.'

'Tilly,' Sol reproved me, 'that bit of bad news was in the last batch sent on by the post office.'

'Was it?'

'You just don't care a fig, do you?'

'No, I don't. Not any more.'

Sol made a great play of rustling letters at me down the phone. 'At least *he's* faithful. He's not giving up.'

'No,' I said. 'I don't suppose I ever really thought he would.'

Sol sighed. 'So what am I supposed to do with all this stuff?'

'The same as last week and the week before. Bank any cheques and burn the crap.'

'And all these billets-doux?'

'Begging letters,' I corrected. 'If I were you, Sol, I'd just gather them up and burn them too. Because they're crap as well.'

'You're a cow, Tilly. Do you know that?'

'Yes. And I've strayed off the range for good.'

'Where *are* you, anyway? Or are you still not telling?'

'That's right, Sol. Still not telling.'

In the end, Geoffrey rented a furnished room only a few streets from the house we'd left. 'He claims it's "quite nicely kitted out, considering",' Sol disapproved down the phone. 'That means that, even though the man no longer has an income, he's going to be paying quite unnecessary storage costs as well as a higher rent for the room.'

'Be fair. He hasn't any furniture of his own.'

'You never took that *too*?'

'It was all mine.'

'Tilly, you're such a *bitch*. If you don't come and sleep with me soon, I'm going to begin to dislike you.' Sol's voice turned serious. 'Actually, I mean it, Tilly. This time you've gone too far, and I can't stand much more of reading these letters.'

'You needn't bother. I only need to know where he is. Just check the address at the top, then shove them in the bin.'

'I can't. They arrive in such pitiful-looking batches. I can't help wanting to know what's going on. And it is painful.' I almost heard him make the decision to press on and say it. 'Tilly, you really should get in touch with him. You ought to get it together to summon enough common charity to put this poor bloke out of his misery once and for all.'

And so I did. I wrote the letter that explained I'd gone for good, and why. With fulsome apologies, I enclosed the very few pieces of Geoff's paperwork I claimed had 'by an oversight' ended up in the wrong van. Somewhere among them, as if by accident, lay a clean copy of the information sheet I'd used as a bookmark in that little hotel, all those long years ago. On one side, photocopied onto fresh paper at one of Mr Stassinopolous's brilliant new Print-It! franchises springing up all over, was the pretty Victorian etching of Lartington Tower itself, with ivy tumbling all over. And on the other there was the little hand-drawn map, unchanged, showing the Folly Edge Hotel, and the way that the roads lay. Of course I'd blotted out the ancient prices and the opening hours and, in their place, put in a reasonable weekly rental charge and, in an assumed hand, the dates booked by 'Ms Tilly Foster'. The end date had been chosen very carefully. I know how Geoffrey ticks. The instant he realized he only had, at most, one day to catch me before I left, he would be up and away. To get the timing how I wanted it, I had no choice but to deliver the package by hand on the right evening. I left it to the very last to shove the whole lot in an old used envelope with a smudged postmark, stick on a label addressed by hand to Geoffrey and, making some excuse about a sprained wrist, even persuade some amiable rambler passing my door to do me the favour of scrawling the words 'Sorry. Package misdelivered next door' across the top.

Then I locked up this nice bright house that overlooks the duck pond, and drove back a hundred miles to the drab little one-eyed town in which I'd thrown away so many years. Without much trouble I found the block of flats into which Geoff had moved so recently. Sol had referred to the area as 'pretty grungy, frankly, if you can judge by the tenants I have in that street'. And I admit that Geoff had certainly come down in the world.

Still, not a problem much longer. Raising my raincoat hood, I left the car and crept down the darkened street. I was quite careful estimating floors and windows. Twice I went softly up and down the communal stair and back outside, to check that that sad blue flicker against the curtains came from a television in the right flat. I still had worries. Push the package through too soon and things might not work out right. Leave it too late and Geoffrey might have got so stuck into his drinking that even he might judge himself unfit to drive.

In the end, I simply had to tell myself, 'Go on, Tilly. Take a chance.' I shoved the package noisily through his letterbox and legged it down the smelly concrete stairs and out of sight round the corner, back to my car, to start the long drive back.

And of course he came after me. That very night. I'd done my homework well. I knew how long it would take him to drive that far down the coast on roads he didn't know. I knew that, by the time he arrived, the tide would be out, exposing the vicious rocks. I knew there'd be no moon. Oh, bad Bad Tilly! I even knew that, if the gate a hundred yards beyond the Folly Edge Hotel had had its padlock removed with wire cutters, and been swung ajar, then anyone trying to follow some little hand-drawn map on a small sheet of paper would almost certainly fail to notice the first of the two warning signs.

Dirt tracks to private properties by the sea are common enough. I knew that wouldn't slow up Geoff when he was so determined to reach me before I left. As for the last sign – DANGER OF DEATH! CLIFF EDGE – well, to be frank, he simply can't have seen it. Is it so bad to lean one giant safety warning against another? And the sign I had smuggled from the company store – YOU BREAK THIS RULE, WE FLY YOU OUT – was, after all, a lot more relevant to the occasion. I do expect he noticed that. But by the time it gave him pause for thought, it was too late. His car was already flying of its own accord off Folly Leap out into solid blackness and down to the rocks, where it burst into flames.

Raking the ashes after, before the tide swept in to wash the mess away, the coastguard may even have come across a few charred scraps of a flyer that had a drawing of the old Lartington Tower. But when the coroner asked himself what Geoff was doing there, the answer seemed clear enough. I'd told them all about my final letter, and Sol had made it perfectly plain I'd only written it in the first place because he'd urged me. As everyone agreed, a woman has every right to leave her partner – especially if she's not married. And when they looked into Geoff's life, even the most ebullient investigating officer could understand how suicidal instincts might trouble a man so very clearly on the way down.

Indeed, they'd been as kind and sensitive as they could be when they had tracked me down.

'An accident? *Dead?* Truly? Oh, how horrible!'

My hands were shaking. (I don't believe they stopped till I had got that warning sign and the wire cutters safely away to the tip.) But both the police officers said it, again and again, 'You mustn't blame yourself.' Sol said the same. 'I know I called you wicked, Til. But really, if the man hadn't got the bottle to keep on going just because you'd given him the final flick, you can't be blamed.' Ed took an even tougher line. 'Don't quote me, Tilly. But personally, I think that suicide's despicable. It heaps so much onto the person who's left.' And Donald's note, enclosing the last few letters, went further. 'It was an aggressive act. Don't let it spoil your new life, Til.'

And they are right, of course. I mustn't blame myself. No one can have it both ways. There can't be one rule for some and another for everyone else. So either Geoff and I were both responsible for every single thing we did – or neither of us had a choice in how our characters made us deal with these matters. I sit here, blissfully happy that honours are even at last. He's paid for twenty years of my life with twenty of his own – even a few more. I smile and watch the ducks and wonder what to do and where to go when I am ready. Sometimes I like to play with the idea that the two of us were both guilty as sin. At other times, I like to think that we were both innocent victims.

One thing at least is true. We are successfully parted at last. And nothing will ever get to spoil that.